LOOK OUT!

The closer Alex got to the watch room and higher observation balcony located directly below the lens area, the more certain he became that something was wrong. He felt a kinship to the tower, as if they shared a common pulse. Something was screaming inside his head that the sentinel was out of balance. When Alex noticed that the door to the lens itself was slightly ajar, the hairs on the back of his neck stood up.

There was no sign that the lock had been forced, but Alex owned the only key, and the door had been securely locked the night before. He climbed the last few steep stairs carefully, then looked out on the narrow walkway that surrounded the top part of the tower.

There was a body lying faceup on the catwalk, the head lolling eerily toward Alex. . . .

MORE MYSTERIES FROM THE BERKLEY PUBLISHING GROUP . . .

CAT CALIBAN MYSTERIES: She was married for thirty-eight years. Raised three kids. Compared to that, tracking down killers is easy . . .

by D. B. Borton

ONE FOR THE MONEY
THREE IS A CROWD
FIVE ALARM FIRE
TWO POINTS FOR MURDER
FOUR ELEMENTS OF MURDER
SIX FEET UNDER

ELENA JARVIS MYSTERIES: There are some pretty bizarre crimes deep in the heart of Texas—and a pretty gutsy police detective who rounds up the unusual suspects . . .

by Nancy Herndon

ACID BATH
LETHAL STATUES
TIME BOMBS
WIDOW'S WATCH
HUNTING GAME
C.O.P. OUT
CASANOVA CRIMES

FREDDIE O'NEAL, P.I., MYSTERIES: You can bet that this appealing Reno private investigator will get her man . . . "A winner."—Linda Grant

by Catherine Dain

LAY IT ON THE LINE
WALK A CROOKED MILE
BET AGAINST THE HOUSE
DEAD MAN'S HAND
SING A SONG OF DEATH
LAMENT FOR A DEAD COWBOY
THE LUCK OF THE DRAW

BENNI HARPER MYSTERIES: Meet Benni Harper—a quilter and folk-art expert with an eye for murderous designs . . .

by Earlene Fowler

FOOL'S PUZZLE
KANSAS TROUBLES
IRISH CHAIN
GOOSE IN THE POND
DOVE IN THE WINDOW
SEVEN SISTERS
MARINER'S COMPASS
ARKANSAS TRAVELER

HANNAH BARLOW MYSTERIES: For ex-cop and law student Hannah Barlow, justice isn't just a word in a textbook. Sometimes, it's a matter of life and death . . .

by Carroll Lachnit

MURDER IN BRIEF
JANIE'S LAW
AKIN TO DEATH
A BLESSED DEATH

PEACHES DANN MYSTERIES: Peaches has never had a very good memory. But she's learned to cope with it over the years . . . Fortunately, though, when it comes to murder, this absentminded amateur sleuth doesn't forgive and forget!

by Elizabeth Daniels Squire

WHO KILLED WHAT'S-HER-NAME?
MEMORY CAN BE MURDER
IS THERE A DEAD MAN IN THE HOUSE?
FORGET ABOUT MURDER
REMEMBER THE ALIBI
WHOSE DEATH IS IT ANYWAY?
WHERE THERE'S A WILL

Innkeeping with MURDER

Tim Myers

BERKLEY PRIME CRIME, NEW YORK

INNKEEPING WITH MURDER

A Berkley Prime Crime Book / published by arrangement with the author

PRINTING HISTORY
Berkley Prime Crime edition / June 2001

For information address: The Berkley Publishing Group, a division of Penguin Putnam Inc., 375 Hudson Street, New York, New York 10014.

The Penguin Putnam Inc. World Wide Web site address is www.penguinputnam.com

ISBN: 0-425-18002-6

Berkley Prime Crime Books are published by The Berkley Publishing Group, a division of Penguin Putnam Inc., 375 Hudson Street, New York, New York 10014.

PRINTED IN THE UNITED STATES OF AMERICA

10 9 8 7 6 5 4 3

For Patty,
Who never stopped believing.

1

"Alex, we've got a problem."

At the sound of the maid's voice, Alex Winston jerked his head up, cracking his skull on the steel pipe placed treacherously just above the opening of the furnace he'd been working on. Alex had been crouched in an awkward position staring at the mysterious workings of the inn's antique boiler, trying unsuccessfully to figure out what was wrong with the blasted thing this time.

For a moment, all Alex could see was a dancing whirlwind of flashing white lights.

"Damn!" he said as he rubbed the crown of his head. No blood came away on his hand, thank God for small favors.

"Are you cursing at me?" Marisa Danton's tone implied that an improper response from Alex would send her fleeing to her room in tears yet again. It had happened too many times to count over the past three months she'd been housekeeping for him at The Hatteras West Inn, an exact replica of the Cape Hatteras

Lighthouse nestled on forty acres of land in the foothills of the Blue Ridge Mountains.

With a forced smile, Alex said, "No, of course not, I would never swear at you." He'd become quite adept at soothing Marisa's ruffled feathers. Alex needed his maid's goodwill, but he also needed a working furnace. Without it, they would both be out of work. Worse yet, Alex could lose the only home he had ever known.

Marisa stared at the mechanical workings of the boiler, a slow smile coming gently to her lips. "It's broken again? That's the third time in two weeks." She looked absolutely delighted by the misfortune.

Alex couldn't figure out what there was to smile about. The cantankerous boiler supplied the heat and hot water for all the guest rooms in the two buildings that made up the inn. It was difficult keeping up two guest buildings as well as the lighthouse, but there really wasn't much choice. The arrangement and construction of the buildings had been determined long before Alex Winston had been born, one stormy Halloween night nearly thirty years before.

Alex kicked the cast-iron base, cracking his big toe with the impact. "I can't believe how ungrateful this mechanical nightmare is. I should have thrown it out years ago."

He looked at the boiler with disgust. He could usually coax the antiquated system back to life with a judicious whack from his monkey wrench, but even his verbal threats to dismantle the oil eater and sink it in the lake down the road had met with no response. On second thought, he realized it wouldn't do to pollute one of the features that drew guests to the inn. The lake, though small by some standards, was large enough to allow visitors to fish from the banks or from a canoe. Alex had gotten a good deal on four battered aluminum canoes from a summer camp that had gone bankrupt the year before. After giving each boat a fresh coat of green aluminum paint, he began offering them to his guests, for a slight fee, of course. Alex used every angle he could think of to generate more income, but no matter how much money he brought in, there never seemed to be enough.

The boiler was a case in point, nothing more than a big black hole waiting to swallow what was left in his dwindling bank account. Still, he had no choice but to have it fixed immediately. Lacking basic amenities, his guests would disappear faster than cotton candy in a thunderstorm. The weather in the foothills of North Carolina could suddenly turn cool during the fall months, and they were now in the heart of autumn.

As gently as he could, Alex asked, "What problem were you talking about when you came in?" Marisa started to answer, but Alex held up his hand to cut off her response. "Never mind, I don't want to know. Marisa, if something's wrong, you're going to have to deal with it yourself. I have to call Mor or Les." The two men operated the town's combination handyman service and fix-it shop. Unfortunately, both men were on intimate terms with his troublesome boiler.

Marisa's lower lip quivered in a rapidly increasing tempo, a sure sign she was fighting back a crying jag. Her teary spells had concerned Alex at first, but he'd soon learned that the girl would cry at the slightest provocation. Barely in her twenties, Marisa had the look of a wild doe, from her long thin body and matching oblong face to the biggest set of brown eyes Alex had ever seen.

Marisa stifled back the tears and mumbled something Alex couldn't understand. He tried to bury his irritation with the girl before he spoke. She hadn't done anything to anger him, but the throbbing ache in his head from the boiler collision was hard to ignore.

In a voice calmer than he felt, Alex said, "Relax and take a deep breath." She did as he suggested, and Alex could see the quivering recede. "There, that's better. Now what's the problem you wanted to tell me about?"

"You said I should handle it myself."

Alex coaxed her gently. "I shouldn't have said that. I'll take care of whatever's wrong."

"It's Mr. Wellington," Marisa said. "He asked me to wake him from his nap, but he won't come to the door no matter how hard I knock. It's time for him to take his medication. I just know he's forgotten again."

"Where's Junior?" It was a ridiculous moniker for a fifty-year-old man, but that was the name Reg Wellington insisted everyone call his grown son. Although the senior Wellington had been vacationing at the mountain lighthouse for as long as Alex could remember, he had never brought his son with him before this trip.

Marisa said, "I can't find him anywhere either. I don't know what to do."

Great, just great. For the hundredth time that day, Alex wished his dad had left him anything but the inn. After his father had died, Alex's brother Tony had opted for cash, and in a burst of sentimentality that Alex had often regretted since, he'd volunteered to take over the ten-room inn and connecting lighthouse where the two of them had grown up.

Rubbing the crown of his head, Alex asked, "Marisa, would you like me to take care of Mr. Wellington myself?"

The maid's face lit up. "Oh would you?" With the glimmer of a smile, she added, "I'll be happy to call Mordecai for you."

So that was the reason she'd been pleased about the boiler trouble; it was another chance for her to see Mor. It was obvious by the way Marisa doted on him that she had a crush on the handyman. Marisa was the only person in Elkton Falls who didn't call Mor by his nickname. Les was the founder and older partner, Lester Williamson. Everyone around town had called them Mor or Les for years, so the two men finally decided to adopt the name officially for their business.

"You do that," Alex told her. "Tell him it's the boiler again." As an afterthought, he added, "You might want to mention that if he doesn't get over here soon, there'll be no money to pay last month's bill."

Alex used every weapon at his disposal to keep the inn open. He'd robbed Peter so many times to pay Paul, Pete was getting absolutely gun-shy.

He followed Marisa out of the mechanical equipment room and walked to the inn's front desk. The check-in space was located in the annex lobby, an area devoted to padded easy chairs, a television and a welcoming fireplace. There were game boards set up along the expanse of front windows where guests could try their hand at Checkers, Chess, Backgammon and Scrabble, though the letter game had become a true challenge ever since an eight-year-old had taken every "E" in the set home with him after his family's visit to the inn.

Marisa stopped to primp her hair in front of a mirror that hung behind the desk before making the call to the handyman. Alex shook his head in bewilderment and took out his master key as he walked to room 10.

Reginald Wellington Senior had been staying there since the days when Alex's father had first opened the inn. For the last two weeks of every September as long as Alex could remember, the older man had occupied the replica of the main keeper's room, lording over the lighthouse like a formidable station master. Alex had a soft spot in his heart for the kindly man. Reg knew more about lighthouses than anyone Alex had ever met, and he hadn't been stingy with his knowledge while Alex had been growing up. The two of them were great friends, sharing a passion that transcended the difference in their ages. This year the senior Wellington had finally persuaded his only son to come along with him on his annual sojourn. Alex didn't care for Junior's stuffed-shirt disposition, but he tried to be polite for Reg's sake.

Alex tapped on the guest room door with a knuckle. "Reg? Are you in there?" He was certain the board members of Wellington Senior's company would be shocked to hear anyone refer to the patriarch as Reg, but it had been a tradition between the two of them since Alex first began to talk.

A hint of concern swept through him. Alex suddenly realized that he had no idea how old Reginald Wellington was. Like the ancient pines and oaks surrounding Alex's land, the man was ageless in his eyes. Reg was as solid and enduring as the granite of Bear Rocks, a conclave of boulders that abutted the lighthouse and was part of his property.

Another knock, and still no response. Alex raised his

voice, as Reg had most likely removed his hearing aid before lying down for his nap. "Get decent. I'm coming in."

Alex slid his pass key into the lock.

Reg wasn't there. In and of itself, that didn't mean anything, but Alex was still concerned. The older man took a nap every afternoon at precisely the same time, and according to Alex's watch, Reg should have only just awakened. He looked carefully around the room. The bed was neatly made, due more to Reg's fastidiousness than Marisa's. As a housekeeper, Marisa was an excellent crier.

The main keeper's chamber, like every other guest room at the inn, featured floors, walls and ceilings made entirely of rich yellow Southern pine. The wood had mellowed over the years to a golden patina, making the space warm and cozy. The windows, large and abundant to catch the cooling breezes of the mountains, were trimmed in white, offering an instant cheery vista to the outside world. Each guest room sported a brightly decorated quilt featuring lighthouses from all over the world. To fight the chill of night, they covered the inn's plain pine Shaker-style beds. Alex's mother and grandmother had made every quilt in the inn, adding to the overall effect that Hatteras West was a home away from home for its guests. All of the furniture sported sleek, clean lines, complementing rather than competing with the textures of the wooden walls. Large floor-to-ceiling fireplaces of faded brick adorned every room, but only the flue in the main lobby downstairs actually worked. One more item on Alex's list of improvements was the restoration of the guest-room fireplaces, but it would have to wait for another, more prosperous day.

Alex locked the door quietly behind him, wondering

where his friend could be. The only other place Reg went during his visits was the top of the lighthouse. That's where Alex would look next.

Alex left the guest building and headed for the lighthouse next door. To him, the lighthouse's older sibling on the Outer Banks was the structure that looked out of place. It appeared downright naked sitting among the scrub pines and the sand dunes. Alex had taken a rare break from the inn to watch them move that lighthouse away from the sea's ever-reaching grasp. Seeing the work the professional crew had undertaken, he'd been darned glad *his* lighthouse was safely tucked away in the mountains.

Alex stroked the granite base lightly as he entered the stairwell and headed up the two-hundred-sixty-eight steel steps that led to the top. Nine landings matched nine windows, offering Alex an excellent view of the nearby mountains.

He peeked out the fourth landing's window and spotted Barb Matthews, a guest of the inn, scurrying along one of the wooded hiking trails that surrounded the property. The one thing Alex had was land, and plenty of it.

He watched Mrs. Matthews dart up the trail, pausing now and then to investigate something on the ground at her feet before hurrying on. She would stoop to pick up small rocks from the path, study them for a moment, then most likely cast them aside into the woods. It was like watching an ardent ant in search of food. Her walking stick stayed firmly in one hand the entire time, though he noticed that the older woman walked perfectly well without it.

Somehow she must have sensed Alex's eyes upon her. Mrs. Matthews tilted her head back and stared directly into the window opening. There was a look of scorn on her face that Alex had grown used to seeing since she'd first started coming to the inn in early May. She was now on her third visit this year, and Alex supposed he should be happy for the business, but truthfully, he didn't care for the grumpy woman.

Alex leaned back out of the window's line of sight and finished his climb toward the watch room and the lantern above.

Great-grandfather Adlai had installed the original Fresnel lens that supplied the lighthouse's strong beam, but he'd rarely used the beacon himself. Alex's father had run it so often at night that the local townspeople had complained about the midnight strobe. The county government acted, passing a special ordinance limiting the operation of the lantern to situations of emergency in the valley.

The commissioners did make one exception to their ruling. A yearly test of the lantern's light had evolved into a celebration for the area. People from seven counties came to picnic at the base of the lighthouse in the growing dusk, and there was always a hushed awe as the current Winston lighthouse keeper flipped on the electricity that now powered the slowly rotating beam. It was one of the moments Alex lived for since taking over the inn from his father.

The closer Alex got to the watch room and higher observation balcony located directly below the lens area, the more certain he became that something was wrong. He felt a kinship to the tower, as if they shared a common pulse. Something was screaming inside his head that the sentinel was out of balance. When Alex noticed that the door to the lens itself was slightly ajar, the hairs on the back of his neck stood up.

There was no sign that the lock had been forced, but Alex owned the only key, and the door had been securely locked the night before. He climbed the last few steep stairs carefully, then looked out on the narrow walkway that surrounded the top part of the tower.

There was a body lying faceup on the catwalk, the head lolling eerily toward Alex.

Reginald Wellington Senior wouldn't be needing his pill after all.

Somehow, he'd managed to get into the highest observation point of the lighthouse on his own. But it appeared that the climb had killed him. One look at Reg's pallid, lifeless face and hollow, empty gaze told Alex that there was no real hurry to call Doc Drake.

His friend had obviously been dead for some time.

2

"Sheriff Armstrong, I need you out at the inn right away." The sheriff had been hanging out at the second place Alex had phoned, a diner called Buck's Grill. To Alex's credit, he'd tried to reach the sheriff at his office in town with his first call.

"Is that you, Alex? What's the rush?" Armstrong asked. In a lower voice, he added, "Is it anything we can handle over the phone? I'm doing a little campaigning at the moment."

"I need you at the lighthouse. This is serious."

Alex's words instantly sobered the sheriff. "Tell me what's going on."

Alex knew the man was a competent sheriff; unfortunately that wasn't all it took to get elected in Canawba County. Armstrong had barely won his primary, and there were doubts around Elkton Falls that he could beat his old crony Hiram Blankenship in the upcoming general election. The only qualification required to run for sheriff was a pulse. Blankenship was the town barber, and really seemed uninterested in being sheriff at all. An argument over what Armstrong still described as the worst haircut of his life had prodded Hiram Blankenship to throw his hat into the political arena and ". . . show that uppity son of a mutt he's not the King of Canawba County." Whatever that was supposed to mean. The way the scissors and clippers had been flying that day, Alex had resolved to let his hair grow long until after the election; it just wasn't safe sitting in the barber's chair during one of Hiram's tirades. Alex had to admit that the barber was more qualified to be sheriff than some of the candidates that county had seen in the past. At least Hiram had been a member of the military police when he'd served his stint in the armed forces.

They would have to hose down the whole county after the November balloting to get rid of all the mud being slung between the two candidates.

Alex paused on the phone for a moment as one of his guests entered the lobby. He wanted to get Reg's body out as discreetly as possible. Out of respect, he wanted to protect his friend from prying eyes. And in the process, just maybe he wouldn't lose all of his paying guests that way. A dead body was an innkeeper's worst nightmare; Alex couldn't bear to think about what it meant to him personally losing Reg.

The sheriff prodded him again. "Get on with it, Alex. What's so all fired important?"

Keeping his voice to a near-whisper, Alex said, "I've got a body up here, and I need you to send someone out to pick it up. It has to be done quietly, Calvin."

Alex almost never used the sheriff's first name, and that finally seemed to get the sheriff's attention as much as the news that there was a body at Hatteras West. "Was it foul play?"

Truthfully, the thought hadn't even occurred to Alex. "I sincerely doubt it. It looks like one of my guests had a heart attack climbing the lighthouse stairs."

The sheriff sounded a little disappointed. "As soon as I round up Doc Drake we'll head out your way. Just in case, though, don't touch anything, Alex."

"I mean it about keeping quiet, okay? I don't want to disturb my other guests any more than I have to. Can you forget the flashing lights and the siren for once?"

Armstrong chuckled. "Come on, Alex. I've got to let folks know I'm out doing my job. It's my duty."

Alex shuddered thinking about the sheriff tearing up the gravel road in front of the inn, driving like a demon possessed and scaring his guests half to death. "How about shutting all the bells and whistles off when you came up Point Road? None of your voters live out here but me."

"Okay, I'll do it your way. Doc Drake just came in the door for lunch. We'll be right out."

After Alex hung up the telephone, he hastily scrawled a "Closed" sign on the back of an old flyer and took a few pieces of Scotch tape from the desk. Grabbing his keeper's key for the lighthouse's main door on the way out, he hurried down the gravel path that led to the tower.

Barb Matthews had her hand on the lighthouse door when Alex shouted out her name. She was dressed in her usual attire: sensible khaki pants, a maroon blouse and the sturdy brown hiking boots she always wore. She didn't wear any makeup that he could see, and her graying hair was tucked up under a badly abused hat. He wondered briefly when the woman had last smiled.

Certainly not since she'd come to Hatteras West.

He called out, "I'm sorry, Mrs. Matthews. We've got to close the lighthouse for a few hours."

The woman spun around and waited impatiently for Alex to join her. When he got within reach, she started tapping him forcefully on the chest with her cherry walking stick. Perched on top of the slender shaft was a cast-metal dragon's head painted an unnatural shade of gold. The expression on the dragon's face reminded Alex of the woman herself. He had to fight the urge to grab the stick out of her hands as she repeatedly prodded him with it. Instead, he stepped back two paces, putting himself safely out of her reach.

She snapped, "Do you care to share with me why in the world you would close the only attraction this dismal place possesses?"

The woman was one customer Alex wouldn't mind losing. She'd done nothing but gripe since she'd first discovered Hatteras West. As usual, upon arriving the day before yesterday, Mrs. Matthews started in with her complaints. Her room had either too much light or not enough. The same was true of her mattress being too hard or too lumpy, and Alex expected to hear about the towels being too rough or too soft next. Marisa had finally refused to go into the old lady's room at all.

But Mrs. Matthews did have a point. There had to be some reason for shutting the lighthouse down so abruptly.

"Ummm, we're doing a routine check of the old kerosene well, and the fumes need to be vented." The

Fresnel light's power had been converted to electricity long ago, but Barb Matthews wouldn't know that.

The old lady jumped off the stoop. "You mean the lighthouse could explode?"

Wonderful. Now he'd have to deal with another rumor. "No Ma'am, it's just a routine inspection," he said calmly. "The smell should be gone by tomorrow morning, if you want to try then."

Pivoting on her heels, the small woman huffed off toward her room. As she was leaving, she took one last shot at Alex. "If I'm still *here* tomorrow, I may come see it."

Alex muttered under his breath, "And if you're not, the drinks will be on the house."

He must have spoken louder than he'd intended. Either that, or the woman's hearing was better than a basset hound's. "Pardon me?"

"I just said, I hope you enjoy your stay here at the lighthouse."

This mollified her slightly. "Good day to you, Mr. Winston."

Alex bolted the entrance door to the lighthouse and stuck his homemade sign up at eye level. That had been too close. A fine mist started to fall as he examined his work, chilling the air quickly, so Alex sought shelter back in the main lobby. Marisa was at the desk, looking slightly concerned.

"I couldn't find him," she said.

Oh blast. How would this hysterical woman take the news of Reg's death? Alex couldn't handle a scene right now with his maid. Calmly, he said, "Never mind. I'm taking care of Mr. Wellington."

Marisa looked startled. "I'd forgotten all about him.

I was talking about Mordecai. He's nowhere to be found, so I left a message for him on his machine." She glanced around the lobby. "Where *is* Mr. Wellington? Did he get his medicine on time?"

Since there were no guests within earshot, Alex decided reluctantly to go ahead and tell Marisa what had happened to their elderly guest. She'd find out sooner or later. Surprisingly, Marisa didn't shed a single tear at the news. There was even a stiffness to her backbone that Alex had never seen before. Maybe she'd turn out to be a real trooper when things got tough. Goodness knew he could use a break.

Her next words canceled any hope Alex harbored of finding a silver lining in that particular cloud. Marisa's voice was strong and clear as she announced, "I quit."

"Come on, Marisa. There's no reason for that. I need you here."

Her voice grew louder, and Alex wondered for a moment if anyone else would be able to hear her. "Alex Winston, I'm not about to stay in a place where people die."

As Marisa hurried to her small room near the main desk, Alex followed her, talking the whole time. "Maybe you should take a few days off, just to get a rest. With pay, of course. When you come back, everything will be just like it was before."

His words had no effect on her. During Alex's pleading, Marisa quietly jammed her few possessions into a worn suitcase that had been tucked under her bed.

"You can't leave me shorthanded like this," he pleaded. "Marisa, there's no way I can run this place without you."

He watched in disbelief as his maid latched her suitcase firmly and headed out the door. Alex followed her out to her car. A beat-up tan Gremlin from the seventies. She got in the driver's side without a word and started the engine. Only when she was ready to pull out of the parking lot did she roll down her window and speak.

"I'll send my cousin out. She's looking for work. That's the best I can do."

Before he could reply, she was spinning her tires on the gravel parking lot, kicking up a billowing cloud of gray dust. Alex had never met Marisa's cousin, but she had to be better than nothing. He hoped.

Alex couldn't do anything about Reg that instant, but he had another pressing problem he *could* do something about. He walked back into the lobby and dialed Mor or Les's business number. It galled him that he had the seven digits memorized.

Mor picked up on the first ring.

Alex said, "I hope this means you're free to do a job for me."

Mor chuckled softly. "I just heard Marisa's message on the answering machine. I'm not surprised you're having trouble with the boiler. I've told you a hundred times it's long past time to replace it."

Alex tapped a pencil on the sparsely signed logbook. "Save the lecture, my friend. Can you come right out and take a look at it?"

"Sure, just let me leave a note for Les. You know, it's getting to the point where I hate coming out to your place. Friendship should only have to go so far."

Alex sighed. "Listen Mor, if I had the money, I'd buy a new boiler. I swear I would."

Mor laughed. "That's not the problem. I'm just getting sick of Marisa hanging around me like a lovesick puppy."

"Then I can guarantee that you won't have that particular problem anymore."

"What's she done now?"

"Mor, it's a long story, and I don't have a whole lot of time. How about if we chat while you're working."

"See you soon then. Maybe we'll have time for a game of Backgammon or two after I finish."

"I wouldn't count on it."

Alex hung up the telephone and looked out the window toward the parking lot. As he stood there waiting for the sheriff to arrive, his mind went back to happier times at the inn when he had been a boy. He couldn't remember things ever being in such a constant state of turmoil as he was growing up. His father never seemed to have the problems he had running Hatteras West, but those had been different times. With a start, he suddenly realized that it had actually been his mother who had dealt with whatever problems that came up. Alex could remember her soft and gentle way of handling difficulties as they arose. Unfortunately, he hadn't inherited that particular skill from her.

It was more than that, though. In the old days, the lighthouse used to draw people in because of its special charm. Now, just thirty miles away, twelve million visitors traveled the Blue Ridge Parkway every year, yet Alex couldn't keep his inn filled with guests half the time.

To most, Hatteras West was just another Carolina oddity.

But to Alex it was home.

In less than six minutes, Sheriff Armstrong pulled up in front of the inn, Doc Drake beside him. The blue lights flashed, but at least the sheriff hadn't used his siren coming in.

Alex glanced nervously around. None of his guests were about.

Maybe it wouldn't be so bad after all.

3

Barb Matthews popped out of nowhere and somehow managed to get to the patrol car ahead of Alex. Before Armstrong could make it out of the cruiser, the woman was tapping incessantly on the sheriff's window with her walking stick.

"Why were you flashing your lights? Is it the gas leak? Is the lighthouse going to explode?"

Armstrong looked warily at the overbearing woman as he swung his door open. "I don't know anything about a leak. I was just testing my lights out on the open road."

Thank goodness for small miracles. Dame Matthews thought every man alive was born a fool, and the sheriff's explanation did nothing to change her mind. She shot Alex a look of disgust, then stormed away onto a nearby wooded path as the sheriff and the doctor got out of the cruiser.

The policeman spoke first. "What's her problem, Alex? I thought she was going to whack me with that stick for a minute." On a taller man, Calvin Armstrong's weight might have been reasonable. But the sheriff was closer to six feet than the nine feet he'd need to have a proprtionate height/weight ratio. The khaki uniform he wore looked like its seams had been reinforced with fishing line to hold in his great bulk.

Alex looked at Barb Matthews' retreating figure and said, "She enjoys stirring things up."

Steven Drake, the small and wiry town doctor, hopped out of the passenger seat and offered a nod to Alex. "I hear you've got a body on your hands?" he said. "Can't be good for business, can it?"

Alex lowered his voice as he spoke, hoping the two men would follow suit. "The man who died is a fellow who's been coming here since before I was born. We were good friends. I guess his heart just wore out on the climb up the lighthouse steps."

The doctor nodded in sympathy. Moving toward the diagonal black and white striped tower, Drake quickly reached the lighthouse's entry door. The other two men had no choice but to follow. The doctor, a vigorous man in his early forties, led every walk he ever took. Alex thought the man would have made a great drum major.

They got to the "Closed" sign on the door, and Armstrong nodded. "I guess it is, for that particular guest."

Alex kept silent, fighting the anger he suddenly felt for the sheriff. It was just sinking in that Reg was gone, not just for another season, but forever. Alex unlocked the door, then stepped out of Doc Drake's way. No sense in having the man try to run him off the stairs.

Alex followed, with Armstrong taking up the rear. It was obvious the sheriff was not used to climbing. He barely made it to the first of the nine landings before he had to stop for a breather.

By the time Alex had climbed the last of the metal steps, the doctor had already managed to turn the body over and start his examination.

Alex said, "Was I right, Doc? It was his heart, wasn't it?"

When Drake turned to face Alex, his expression was stern and cold. "What's keeping the sheriff?"

"He's taking a break, but he should be right along. Why, what is it?"

Drake shook his head sadly. "Your friend didn't have a heart attack, Alex. Somebody jammed an ice pick into the base of his neck. Pretty nasty business. The poor fella never had a chance."

Alex couldn't believe it. "It's murder? Are you sure? Who'd want to kill Reg?"

Drake turned back to the body. "That's going to be up to the sheriff to decide. There's no doubt it was foul play. Lean down here a second with me. See that entry wound? Someone jammed some kind of skewer in right there."

Alex could see the clotted blood at the base of Reg's neck now that he had been turned over.

The sheriff must have heard some of the conversation between the two men above him. He burst onto the upper balcony, his face red from exertion. "Did I hear you boys say something about murder?"

Drake nodded. "Unless Alex's friend managed to stab himself in the back of the neck and then throw the ice pick away before he died, I'd say that's about right."

Armstrong removed his hat, now soaked with sweat,

and wiped the top of his bald head. "Well I'll be. I solve this one, and I'm sure to be reelected."

Alex asked, "I don't suppose there's any way to keep this quiet now, is there?"

Armstrong shrugged as he said, "Sorry Alex. It's out of my hands. We're going to have to have an official police investigation." He turned to the doctor. "You're willing to sign the death certificate as foul play?"

"That's what I said, you gore hound. Have a little respect for the dead, will you?"

"Sorry, I didn't mean anything by it," Armstrong said apologetically. "Alex, I'll have to shut down the lighthouse until I can get my forensic team over here and dust for prints."

Alex was confused for a moment. "You mean your cousin Irene? Don't you think the state police should be in on this? You might need more help than a beautician who freelances as a crime scene specialist."

Armstrong frowned. "She's taken all of the required courses, Alex. On our budget, we're lucky to have her."

Alex wondered how qualified Irene really was, but she was the only option. "Get her over here quickly then. I don't want to leave the lighthouse shut down any longer than I have to. It's the only real attraction I've got."

Armstrong smiled slightly and nodded. "I'll trot right down and call her now." The big man flew down the stairs two at a time. He seemed much more spry now that he was investigating a murder.

Doc Drake stayed with Alex on the balcony. "You thought a lot of this fellow, didn't you?"

Alex kept his eyes off Reg's body. "He taught me

more about lighthouses than my own father did. He was a good man, Doc."

Drake patted Alex's shoulder as the two men looked off into the surrounding hills in silence. Alex kept watching the clouds as they rolled in waves toward him. He loved the sky, and the views his lighthouse offered. Now it looked like his days of enjoying the vista would be tainted forever with the memory of Reg's dead body sprawled on the upper platform.

Alex turned away and started down the steps, suddenly needing to get away from Reg's body. Drake followed silently; there was obviously nothing else he could do there.

Once they were back on the ground, Alex realized that Armstrong had driven away in the patrol car, leaving the doctor stranded at the inn.

Doc Drake said, "I'll bet he left without giving me a second thought, heading off to collect Irene, no doubt. Well, it's no bother. I'll catch a ride with the ambulance boys later. I'd better call Madge and let her know I'm going to be a while."

"You can use the telephone in my room, if you need some privacy."

They walked through the lobby of the inn and back to Alex's spartan private living space. It was a mirror image of Marisa's room, the two having been long ago carved out of a single room.

As Drake went to the telephone, Alex said, "Why don't I get us some coffee?"

The doctor nodded as he picked up the receiver. Alex shut the door softly, giving the doctor a little privacy to talk with his nurse. Madge King had started working for Drake a few months ago as his nurse and secretary when Mrs. Wembly, a stern older woman Drake had inherited with the practice, had retired.

His new assistant had been the only nurse Drake had interviewed who'd been willing to work in the foothills of the North Carolina Mountains. She and the doctor had hit it off immediately, and there were rumors that wedding bells would soon be heard in the hills. Alex would probably use the nuptials as an excuse to fire up the Fresnel lens. Drake would love the gesture; he was a huge fan of the lighthouse himself.

Alex filled the coffee cups from the lobby urn and headed to one set of deck chairs on the front porch of the annex. For a change, none of his guests were hanging around the inn; even Barb Matthews had made herself scarce.

Alex's thoughts kept going back to Reg. Who in the world would have any reason to kill that lovable old man? Alex was ashamed his thoughts went immediately to Junior. He wondered where Reg's son was, and who would tell him about his father. Alex decided he would try to find Junior after Drake left so he could see the man's reaction to the news of his father's death.

Could someone else have lanced Reg? An unrequited love perhaps? The only female on the premises even close to Reg's age was Barb Matthews. The thought of his friend in the arms of someone like that dragon lady made Alex shudder. Surely Reg had better taste than that, but love did strange things to people.

Drake came out onto the porch, interrupting Alex's musings. "Madge is fussing at me for goofing off. She even threatened to drive out and pick me up herself if I don't show up pretty soon." Drake chuckled softly to himself. It was clear to Alex that the doctor enjoyed the attentions of his nurse.

Drake changed the subject. "Now what's on your mind, Alex? If you'd like to talk about it, I've been told I'm a pretty good listener."

Alex hesitated, then realized that it would feel good to get his troubles off his chest.

"I'm fed up, Steven. In the three seasons since I've been operating this place on my own, I've had nothing but trouble. Dad never had my run of bad luck in all the years he ran Hatteras West. I'm starting to wonder if I'm cut out for the innkeeper's life after all. Maybe my brother was the smart one to take the money and run."

Drake gestured to the cars in the parking lot. "You seem to be doing pretty well."

Alex shook his head. "To tell the truth, I'm barely scraping by. Marisa left the second she found out about Reg's death, and the boiler is out of whack again. I'm tempted to take Sam Finster's advice, sell the place and be done with it."

Sam Finster was the area's local real estate whiz. He'd been after Alex to sell the lighthouse and the accompanying keeper's houses for the past four months.

Finster didn't fight fair, either. When Alex had refused the agent's third offer during the first weeks of his attempted negotiation, Finster started a campaign of lies around town so that Alex's neighbors would join in pressuring him to sell. The latest rumor making the rounds was that an amusement conglomeration wanted to add Lighthouse Land to its inventory of attractions. The lie changed weekly, but Alex still had no idea who the real prospective buyer was.

The worst part of all was that the agent himself had

spread this latest rumor around town, telling everyone what a great thing the proposed amusement part would be for the community. The idea of jobs and tourists appealed to many of the people who lived in Elkton Falls and the rest of Canawba County. Everybody wanted to cash in on those tourists dollars. Several of the townsfolk had even started snubbing Alex on his trips into town.

The doctor snorted in disgust. "Don't let that vulture get his claws into you. Tell me the truth. You aren't going to sell, are you? Hatteras West is a part of you; it's obvious to anyone with eyes that you love this place."

Alex nodded, staring up at the faded black and white stripes of the lighthouse. "God help me, I do. I don't know what I'd do if—."

Their conversation was interrupted by the sound of a truck coming up the gravel road. Alex recognized Mor's fix-it shop on wheels. Mordecai Pendleton slid on the loose gravel, barely managing to stop the truck three inches from the concrete bumpers Alex had put in specifically to keep the man from driving straight into the main keeper's house.

As he climbed out of the truck, Mor gave the two men a big wave. "Hey Doc. Alex, if I had kids, that boiler of yours would be putting them through college."

Alex grinned in spite of himself. Mor Pendleton always had a way of cheering him up. The fix-it man looked like a linebacker, which he had indeed been in college. An illegal late hit had resulted in two bad knees during his junior year, sending Mor back to his old hometown minus his scholarship and without enough money to finish his degree. A lesser man might have spent his time dreaming of the glory and the paychecks that could have been, but Mor was the happiest man Alex knew.

Alex said, "I don't have to show you the way, do I? I'd like to talk to Doc a bit longer."

Mor retrieved his tool kit and slapped Alex on the back. "You mean you're not going to watch? Jeez, buddy, in that case I can give you a price break if I don't have to work with an audience." Without another word, the big man walked through the doors toward the complex's utility room.

Less then a minute later, Alex saw the police cruiser return up the driveway. He could clearly see Irene sitting in front, her red beehive hairdo at least forty years behind the times. From where Alex stood, there appeared to be a strange woman in back of the car.

Armstrong popped out of the cruiser and smiled. "I've got somebody who says she's got a job out here. Claims Marisa Danton sent her." Heading up the lighthouse stairs, Armstrong, Irene, and Drake left the two of them alone.

Alex had forgotten all about Marisa's cousin. The last thing he wanted was to saddle himself with another Danton, but he really didn't have any choice. It was barely possible for two people to run the inn. He knew he couldn't manage without help. Alex just hoped this particular cousin didn't have the same tearful tendencies Marisa had.

As she got out of the car, Alex was surprised to see that the girl was extraordinarily attractive. Long, lustrous chestnut hair hung past her shoulders, highlighting her gentle green eyes. Unlike Marisa, this woman possessed a fullness to her figure that Alex had always preferred over the gaunt, underfed type. Her ample curves were well defined in her blue jeans and burgundy short-sleeved T-shirt. As pretty as she was, Alex figured this little beauty probably wouldn't lower herself to scrub the toilets or make beds. Still, it wasn't like he had many options. Gamely, he went over to greet her as she pulled a single, well-worn suitcase from the cruiser's backseat.

Alex introduced himself. "I'm Alex Winston, owner and proprietor of Hatteras West."

She smiled softly as she took his hand. "I'm Elise Danton, it's nice to meet you. Marisa told me you were looking for someone, and I'd like to apply for the job."

Still shaking the girl's hand, Alex said, "You're hired."

Elise pulled her hand back abruptly. "You're not some kind of wolf, are you?"

Alex spread his open hands out in a show of innocence. "We won't know that until the next full moon, will we? You should be perfectly safe until then."

Elise wasn't buying it for a second. "Then why are you hiring me so quickly?"

It was obvious she was immune to his attempt at charm as he explained, "Well, it's not that tough a job, so I don't doubt you can do it. Plus, you're Marisa's cousin, so I don't have to check your references, and finally, you're the only one applying for the job." He shrugged. "What can I say. I'm desperate."

"That I understand. Let's get started." She was all business.

He asked, "Would you like a tour of the place first?"

Elise shook her head. "I can find everything I need on my own. Just show me the cleaning supplies, and I'll take it from there. I understand you've got quite a lot on your plate as it is today."

Alex breathed a sign of relief. Elise already impressed him more than Marisa ever had. There was an air of competence about her, a familiarity, that made Alex feel hopeful for the first time in quite a while that things at Hatteras West had a chance of improving.

4

It took Alex less than ten minutes to get Elise settled into her new job. That was remarkable in itself, based on how long it had taken Marisa to get acclimated. His new maid, armed with a set of keys and a cart full of supplies, headed off to clean the first room on her list.

Alex walked back to the utility room to see if Mor was having any luck with the boiler.

The big man was putting the last of his tools back into his steel tool chest.

Alex groaned. "Oh, no. Don't tell me it's hopeless. You've at least got to try."

Mor offered him a huge grin. "Come on, Alex, lighten up. I've already taken care of the problem. You got lucky today, but I wouldn't bet on it next time."

Alex thought of Reg's body at the top of the lighthouse and of the impact it would have on his guests, wondering just how lucky he could be. "Does this mean we have hot water?"

Mor said, "Give the boiler a few minutes to get

warmed up, and you'll be back in business. I bet that water is freezing straight out of the well."

Alex watched with trepidation as Mor began to fill out a bill. Alex must have caught his friend's eye, because when the handyman looked up from his paperwork, Mor was grinning broadly.

"I didn't need any parts, all I had to do was adjust the air intake valve. I'd teach you to do it yourself, but then where would I be without all these hefty fees I charge you? All you have to pay for today is my labor. Les said something about collecting up front, since Marisa threatened on the answering machine to stick us with your bill from last month."

Alex tried to return his grin, but couldn't manage it. "I don't blame you a bit for asking. I just hope I have enough to cover it. How much do I owe you?"

Mor made a careful study of his watch. "Well, I'll be. I've been on my own time since I left the shop. How about if I tell Les the boiler fixed itself? That and a cold beer, we'll call it even."

"That sounds like a deal to me. Thanks, I really appreciate it, Mor."

Maybe Alex *was* due to have a little good luck come his way. More likely, his luck came from having Mor as a good friend. The two of them had grown up together in Elkton Falls; they'd even been on the high school football team together when Mor was a senior and Alex was a sophomore. While Alex wasn't nearly as good as his friend on the gridiron, he'd still been enough of a ballplayer to make the all-county squad during his own senior year, albeit as a member of the third team.

Alex walked Mor back into the lobby where they

both happened to catch a glimpse of Elise entering a guest room on the first floor.

Mor whistled softly. "That is one sweet heartbreaker you've got on your hands there. Since when did Elise sign on at the inn? When you said Marisa was gone, I had no idea you'd set your sights so high on your next maid. Not that I blame you. I'd work side-by-side with that young lady any day of the week."

Alex said brusquely, "She needs a job, and I happened to have an opening. Do you know much about her?"

Mor's eyes twinkled. "Not nearly as much as I'd like to. From what I hear, she's just been in town a few weeks. I ran into her over at the grocery store. Asked her out right off the bat, too; some opportunities are too good to pass up."

Alex knew Mor was famous throughout seven counties as a heartbreaker in his own right. Fathers had been known to send their eligible daughters out on phantom errands before calling Mor for a job, just to be sure they were well out of the handyman's reach.

"So what did she say when you asked her out?"

The big man chuckled softly. "She was polite enough, but I got the message pretty fast that she wasn't interested."

Alex smiled gently at his friend. "I'll bet you were floored. Is that the first time you've ever been turned down?"

Mor slapped him on the back. Alex couldn't believe how much the harmless-looking tap stung. "Well, she told me she was engaged, that's what made the message loud and clear. What are you worried about? You're still dating Sandra, aren't you?"

"Off and on," he admitted. Sandra Beckett was a lawyer from town Alex went out with occasionally. They kept it casual, no real strings between them, which suited Alex just fine.

Alex added, "To be honest with you, I need a maid a lot more than I need a new girlfriend. I've got my guests to consider, you know."

Mor nodded his head a little too vigorously. "Yeah, right. I always knew you were a fine one to look out after your guests. Now how about looking after me for a minute? I'd still like that beer."

Alex led his friend back to his own modest quarters and retrieved a cold beer from the dormitory-sized refrigerator. Alex had taken for himself the inn's only room without a fireplace. Since taking the space over it had become his own little nook where he could temporarily get away from the constant demands of running the inn. There was a sampler quilt hanging on the wall at the head of his bed that his mother had made. She had loved to tell the story of how Alex had come to her on a Halloween night in the middle of a rare hurricane appearance in Elkton Falls. It was their special bond, surviving the storm together, and Alex missed his mother terribly. He and his father had been close, but their relationship had been nothing like the one he'd had with his mother. Alex wondered briefly if his father was haunting the place, making sure his son stayed on his toes.

It would have been just like him.

Alex took an extra beer out of the refrigerator for himself and the two men headed for one of the Backgammon boards set up in one corner of the lobby. It was an odd time to be playing a game, but he couldn't face dealing with Reg's death. Worst of all, Alex didn't want to see them carry the body down the steel steps.

Mor set his hulking frame in one of the chairs and took a white game piece off the board. "Pick a hand. Better yet, you can play white, and I'll still beat you like a drum."

Alex suddenly shook his head. "To tell you the truth, I don't much feel like playing. I forgot. You haven't heard what happened, have you?"

Mor dropped the white piece back on the game board. "What's going on?"

Alex brought his friend up-to-date on what had happened at the inn. When he got to the part about finding Reg's body, Alex had to pause to steel himself enough to deliver the words. It was finally sinking in. Reg was really gone.

"So that's what Sheriff Strong-arms was in such an uproar about. I heard him ripping around town right before I headed out your way. That man is a menace in his patrol car. Wonder how many wrecks he's caused himself?

Alex shrugged, suddenly too disheartened to rise to the bait.

Mor got up from his seat and said, "Tell you what. Why don't we take a raincheck on that game of backgammon? I've got some errands to run in town, and I don't want to be late for class."

Alex nodded as he got up from his seat. "What are you studying this time?"

Mor said, "I'm taking photography this semester, and my homework's due tonight. I brought my camera so I could snap some photos on the way back to town. I want to get a few shots of the lighthouse and the inn before I leave."

"Be my guest."

Mor and Alex had enrolled in an adult education class together a few years back, figuring it would be an excellent place to meet single women and perhaps learn something while they were at it. After a great deal of debate, they had settled on a Chinese cooking class. The first night of class, the only woman in the room had been Mrs. Hurley, the high school's home economics teacher for the last fifty years. There were seventeen men enrolled, and not a single woman. Many of the men dropped out the first night, having failed to find any eligible women, but Alex and Mor figured that since they were already there and they'd paid their tuition fees, it couldn't hurt to learn something new. Mor was still taking classes every quarter, finding that he enjoyed learning new things more than sitting around during the evening drinking beer with his old buddies from high school, reliving glory days long gone. Alex joined him in some of the classes during the off-times for the inn, but he still had the fall leaf season ahead of him, one of his busiest times of the year.

Alex watched Mor take a few quick pictures, then walked his friend to his truck.

After Mor was gone, Alex stood in silence staring at the tower, trying to decide whether he wanted to head up to the top of the lighthouse and see how Irene was doing or go back inside and get some paperwork done. He was still debating the pros and cons when Irene, Doc Drake and Sheriff Armstrong came through the lighthouse's paired red doors.

The sheriff walked over to him and said, "Don't

worry about a thing, Alex, Irene says you can have the lighthouse back as soon as the boys from the county come to retrieve the body."

By then, Irene and Doc Drake joined the two of them. Alex turned to Irene, who was, as always, fussing with her hair. Evidently, she wasn't used to climbing stairs, because her pillar of curls was threatening to crash down over her eyes from all the activity.

She pinched his cheek. "You're getting cuter every day, young man. Why don't you have a wife yet? I see you all over town with Sandra Beckett. Anything happening there?"

Alex shrugged, feeling his face redden slightly. Armstrong stepped in and saved him from replying.

"Investigator, we're on a case. I'd appreciate it if you wouldn't harass a potential witness."

Irene rolled her eyes at her cousin, reminding Alex of a ten-year-old instead of the sixty-year-old woman standing before him. "Ducky, why don't you lighten up a little."

It was Armstrong's turn to redden. The story around town went that, as a toddler, he'd become so attached to a yellow plastic duck that he carried it everywhere with him. The name "Ducky" was obviously one the sheriff hoped the town would forget. Most of them had, with the one glaring exception of Irene.

Alex asked, "What did you find out?"

Irene nodded. "Okay, let's get down to business. The murder was pretty much what Doctor Drake thought; a thin sharpened wire was jammed into the victim's neck." She paused, then said. "With all the traffic you get climbing the steps, it was impossible to pull a legible print off the railing. Sorry I didn't have any luck.

About the only thing out of the ordinary I found up there was a handful of rocks."

Doc Drake, who seemed to have a real fondness for the beautician, said, "They most likely fell out of the deceased's pockets. We can't expect you to find clues when there aren't any around, now can we? You did good work up there, Irene, don't let it bother you."

She offered the physician a bright smile and a quick peck on the cheek. Seeing the red brand from her lipstick, Irene took her hankie out and scrubbed the doctor's face clean. "We can't have that pretty new nurse thinking things, now can we?"

Irene turned to her cousin. "I'll be in the car while you men have your chat. Hurry up, Ducky. I've got to give Mrs. Anderson a perm in twenty minutes. Career women these days don't even have time to get their hair done. It's disgraceful, I'm telling you. After you drop me off, you can go over to the One-Hour Photo lab and develop the pictures I took of the crime scene."

Alex turned to the sheriff and said, "Any idea when the ambulance is going to get here?" The thought of Reg's body on the upper balcony was beginning to make Alex nauseous.

"I'll radio over and see what's keeping them." While Armstrong was in the squad car making his call, Drake spoke softly to Alex. "I've got the feeling we'll never find out who did this, or why. The modern world is filled with random acts of violence. The only thing that surprises me is that it took so long to come to our little town here."

Alex shook his head. "I don't think there was anything random about Reg's death, Doc, but I agree that Armstrong might never find out who the real killer is."

Drake said heavily, "Don't sell Armstrong short. I've seen him at work a lot more than you have. He's got a decent mind, and when he gets to thinking about a murder he doesn't think about anything else. If anybody has a chance to figure this out, it's him. Armstrong's the kind of man who thrives under tense situations. It's the normal aspects of life he doesn't handle all that well."

Alex wondered if the sheriff was as competent as the doctor supposed.

He suddenly knew in his heart that he couldn't afford to take that chance. Who would knowingly stay at an inn where a murder had recently taken place? And without paying guests, Hatteras West would die as surely as Reg had. Alex had to face the fact that finding the murderer himself was the only way he could save the inn.

Armstrong rejoined them. "There was a big accident up on Route 70, so they're going to be late. Do you mind if I run Doc and Irene into town, Alex? I'll be back before the ambulance gets here."

Alex nodded. "Fine by me."

As the sheriff walked to his car, he said, "You might want to lock those doors again. "We don't want anybody wandering upstairs."

Alex agreed and did as the sheriff asked. After securely locking the doors, he watched in silence as the squad car disappeared from view. As he turned to head back up the path to the main part of the inn, Alex saw movement in one of the bushes planted near the annex's side porch. By the time he got over to the spot, whoever had been standing there quietly eavesdropping had gone. Alex had a feeling in the pit of his stomach that whoever had murdered Reg Wellington was not going to be satisfied with just one body. He was going to have to do everything he could to be sure the killer didn't have the opportunity to strike again.

5

Just as Alex reached for the knob, one of his guests opened the front door. Joel Grandy looked like everybody's favorite grandfather, from his portly frame and silver hair to the craggy lines of his face. This was his first visit to Hatteras West, but it hadn't taken Alex long to get to know the outgoing man. A recent widower, Joel was touring the country in an effort to rediscover himself. He'd told Alex on the first day of his visit that he had spent sixteen months watching cancer slowly, painfully destroy his wife of thirty-four years. When death had finally come for her nine weeks ago, he'd embraced it as a welcome friend, a final relief to her heroic struggle.

At least the man didn't have money problems added to his personal grief. Joel was wearing an expensive and obviously custom-made suit. Several large diamonds glittered from the gold rings adorning his massive fingers.

His eyes lit up when he spotted Alex. "Just the fellow I've been looking for. I understand there's been a bit of trouble around here."

Alex's heart sank. It looked like the news of Reg's death had already gotten out. Still, it wouldn't do to assume anything. "Trouble?"

Joel grinned. "That crazy bird Matthews cornered me in the hallway. She said something about the lighthouse being shut down."

"That's true enough."

He could feel Joel's gaze studying him. "It's surely not a gas leak. You told me the power supply had been converted to electricity thirty years ago. What's up? You can tell me, lad."

Alex knew he couldn't keep the truth from his guests any longer, not with a murderer possibly still loose on the grounds. "I'm afraid something tragic has happened. Somebody murdered Reg Wellington."

Joel walked over to one of the porch rockers and sat down heavily. Alex joined him.

The older guest stared at the floorboards for a few moments before speaking again. "Who'd want to kill that old codger? We had a chess game scheduled for tonight after dinner."

Alex had seen the two men engaged in a heated discussion over a game the night before. They appeared to take their chess seriously, and Alex had been forced to step in to prevent a brawl in the lobby. Could tempers have flared enough to cause murder?

Trying to sound casual, Alex said, "When's the last time you saw Reg, Joel?"

His guest thought about it a full minute before answering. "He was going to the lighthouse tower two or three hours ago. I happened to be looking out my window and I saw him go inside."

"And you didn't see him after that?" Alex asked.

Joel looked at Alex carefully. "I don't like the direction this conversation is heading. You're not accusing me of anything are you, Alex?"

Alex bit his lip. If Joel had murdered Reg, he'd needed to be more careful in his questioning. "No, I was just wondering if you might have seen anyone else. You must have been the last person to see him alive."

"Besides the murderer, you mean."

Alex nodded in agreement, then said, "I knew Reg for a long time. I just want to be sure that whoever killed him is found."

The suspicion left Joel's face, replaced by sympathy. "I'd forgotten about you two being friends. Reg mentioned how much he wished Junior had turned out more like you. To answer your question, no, he was alone when I saw him. It's a damn shame, that's what it is."

The two men sat in silence for a few moments, then Joel popped out of his chair. The older man did everything with vigor, and Alex suspected that if Joel had committed the murder, he would have acted with more passion, attacking his victim head-on. Stabbing from behind was a sneaky way to murder someone, and Alex had a hard time believing it was a method this particular guest was capable of. But Alex was the first to admit that he'd been wrong before.

Joel said, "Well, you know what they say. Life goes on. I'm heading into town for a bite to eat and some entertainment."

Surprised by his guests's sudden shift in mood, Alex

said, "Joel, under the circumstances, I'll understand if you want to cancel the rest of your stay here."

Joel said, "Are you shutting the inn down?"

"No, of course not. It's just that—."

"Alex, my boy, if you're willing to put up with me, I'm going to hang around a little longer. I'm not afraid of dying." He winked at Alex. "I've got too much going on right now to check out of this lovely inn or of my life." As he walked out to his late-model Lincoln, Joel added with a wink, "Don't wait up for me tonight, I just might be late."

One thing was certain; Joel didn't seem to be wasting any tears over the death of his new friend. Maybe watching his wife die had taught him to deal with death better than most. Or maybe Joel Grandy wasn't all he said he was. Alex was still thinking about the older man when Junior walked up the path toward the keeper's quarters.

Alex would have to break the news to him that someone had jammed a blade into his father's neck.

Studying the man, he searched for the right words. Junior looked like he'd been outfitted from L. L. Bean's wilderness catalogue. From his high-top leather boots to his khaki safari hat, he was more suited to explore the great uncharted depths of Africa than the relatively tame Blue Ridge Mountains.

Junior dropped down with a loud sigh in the rocking chair Joel had just vacated. "What a hike! I've been gone four hours and I didn't think I'd ever make it back."

"You did the loop trail?"

Junior nodded once, emptying the last sip from the canteen clipped onto his belt.

Four hours, for a three-mile hike? "What in the world took you so long?"

Junior looked sheepish. "Don't tell *him,*" he gestured to the upstairs room his father had recently occupied, then explained, "I was studying a clump of wilderness off the path, and the sun was so warm . . . I . . . I must have fallen asleep."

Alex had a hard time believing that. He supposed it was possible Junior could have taken a nap on the trail as he said, but there were no signs that his clothes had been slept in. Alex couldn't see a speck of dirt or a grass stain anywhere on Junior; the outfit looked brand new.

Alex took a deep breath, then announced somberly, "I'm sorry to be the one to tell you this, but your father's dead. I found him at the top of the lighthouse."

Junior's face didn't exactly turn ashen—his complexion was already pasty white, but his eyes did grow large at the news, and he jerked backwards in the chair.

"My God! What happened? Was it his heart? I warned him about climbing those stairs, but he never would listen to me. Mr. Winston, I'm holding you personally responsible for his—."

Alex tried to keep his voice calm as he interrupted. "It's not what you think. I guess I didn't make myself clear. Someone murdered your father."

The news rocked Junior back even farther. Alex worried that the man would topple over in the chair before he managed to steady himself. Junior's surprise was either sincere or very well rehearsed. "Who . . . I don't understand. Do they know who killed him? Why would somebody do that? How did he die?"

Alex chose to answer the latter question first, since he didn't have a clue as to the who or the why. "It appears that he was stabbed in the back of the neck. The doctor says it's most likely he didn't suffer, if that's any consolation."

Junior shook his head. "Oh, my Lord. What am I going to tell the board?"

Alex watched the man closely as he said," I suppose this means you'll be taking over your father's duties at the company immediately."

Junior nodded numbly. "I never wanted it to happen this way."

He started to get up, then plopped back down heavily. In a shaking voice, Junior asked, "I don't suppose you have a shot of something around here, do you? I could really use a drink to steady my nerves."

Alex was ashamed of himself. Instead of playing detective, he should be comforting his guest. It wasn't his job to separate the innocent from the guilty, but it *was* up to him to take care of his guests, no matter what his suspicions were. "If you like bourbon, I've got some Maker's Mark in my room. I'll be right back."

He left Junior alone on the porch and headed inside. Elise was at the front desk studying the sign-in book. When she saw Alex, she was obviously startled, a little like she'd been caught with her hand deep in the cookie jar.

Elise said, "I hope you don't mind me looking at the guest registry. I just wanted to see if there were any more rooms to clean. Can you think of anything else I should do around here?"

"I don't have any secrets from you, Elise. You're welcome to look at everything and anything here. You could do me a favor, though."

Elise asked warily, "What's that?"

"I've got a despondent man out front who just lost his father. It's Reg's son. His name's Junior, believe it or not. Could you take him a drink and get him off the front porch? The ambulance should be here any minute, and I don't want him to have to sit there watching while they cart off his father's body."

Elise nodded immediately, a look of sympathy crossing her face. "I'll take care of it."

Alex retrieved the bottle, two-thirds full, and handed it to Elise. "Thanks. I appreciate you helping out around here on such short notice."

"No problem," she said as she filled a single plastic glass from her housekeeper's cart, then headed outside to the porch.

Alex watched her walk through the door, then glanced down at the registry. It was turned to the week's current guests, and Alex felt a tug in his chest when his eyes fell upon Reg's name.

Elise walked back inside a minute later with Junior in tow, the two of them looking rather chummy.

A moment later Alex saw an unfamiliar car drive up. When a large, heavyset woman somewhere in her forties got out of the red Subaru wagon, he realized that it must be Emma Sturbridge. With only ten rooms split between the two houses, Alex usually had a pretty good idea of who was coming and going each night. In the rush surrounding Reg's death, her scheduled arrival had completely slipped his mind.

Walking out to meet the handsome woman, Alex introduced himself and asked if she was Mrs. Sturbridge.

She took his hand with a grin. "Emma, please. Business must be bad if the owner himself is greeting visitors. I must say I'm flattered by the attention, though."

Alex liked the woman immediately. There were deep laugh lines around her eyes and the corners of her mouth. Dressed in brand-new denim jeans and a man's golf shirt, she exuded an air of delight with the world around her. The smile on her face was genuine and inviting.

Alex said, "I'm not trying to discourage you, but there's been a murder here today. If you'd like to find other accommodations, I'd be happy to refund your deposit and see if I can find another place for you to stay tonight."

Emma studied him for a moment before answering. "Alex, I'm from Washington D.C. Something like murder isn't going to put me off my rockhounding. Have you had any big gem strikes around here lately?"

"Not that I've heard. You're a little far from Hiddenite to be looking for emeralds, aren't you?"

Emma winked. "I've got a theory of my own about the geologic formations around here, so if you'll put me up, I'm willing to take my chances with your bad guy. Over the years I've learned to watch out for myself." The smile vanished for a moment. "I lived with Harold Sturbridge for nineteen years, and he never managed to lay a glove on me in all that time."

Alex took the bag out of Emma's hands. "In that case, I'm pleased to have you stay with us. Welcome to Hatteras West."

After they walked inside and picked up Emma's key, Alex offered to show her to room 8. She grabbed her suitcase out of his hands and said, "Just point me in the general direction, and I'll find my own way."

He gestured down the corridor and watched her easy, loping gate as she headed to her room. Emma Surbridge's warmth and charm would be a welcome addition to the guest list at Hatteras West.

What was keeping the sheriff? Alex walked out onto the porch and was rewarded with the view of the ambulance driving up, Armstrong right behind them in his squad car. At least they weren't traveling with their sirens blaring.

Alex walked out to meet them as they parked. Armstrong pointed the attendants toward the lighthouse, and Alex saw they were carrying a lightweight aluminum stretcher between them. A discreet gray blanket was tucked into the frame. They'd be able to cover Reg's body on the way out.

The sheriff walked over to Alex. "Anybody disturb the body?"

Alex said, "Not that I know of. It's been—"

One of the attendants yelled from the lighthouse base, "Hey Sheriff, this place is locked. How are we supposed to get inside?"

Armstrong turned to Alex and said, "I need the key, if you don't mind."

Alex took the old-fashioned skeleton key off his ring, handed it over, asking, "Is it a good idea to move the body before the state police get here?"

"Alex, I don't call the State Bureau of Investigation every time something happens in Canawba County. I can handle it myself. Hold on a second, could you? I want to talk to you. I'll be right back."

After handing the key to the attendants, Alex heard Armstrong ask, "You'all need any help?"

"No, we can handle it."

As they disappeared through the doorway, Armstrong asked, "Have you given any thought as to who could have done this? I've got a feeling one of your guests might be a murderer."

"Come on, Sheriff, you know how many folks from town use the lighthouse as a Stair Master. While you're naming suspects, you might as well use the county telephone book."

The sheriff mopped away a line of perspiration that had formed on his brow. The man sweated more than anyone Alex had ever known. Or maybe it wasn't just the heat; it could be the pressure he was under to solve the case, and solve it quickly. He said, "You've got a point about it being anybody, but I figure the only people around here who knew him well enough to want to kill him were guests, too. It makes sense, doesn't it?"

When Alex nodded his agreement, the sheriff continued, "Have you looked around the base of the lighthouse for the knife?"

"I've got an inn to run. I haven't had time to play detective," Alex said abruptly, feeling guilty that he'd been doing just that.

Armstrong patted Alex on the shoulder. "Take it easy, Alex, I was just asking. Why don't you take a walk with me around the tower, and we'll have a chance to talk about what really happened."

The grass around the tower's base had just received its monthly trim two days previously. If Reg's murder had occurred three days earlier, they wouldn't have been able to find the blade with a metal detector, the weeds had grown so high. Now, it was simple to walk over the manicured grass and search for the weapon.

As they walked, the sheriff discussed the possibilities. "We've got several ways we can look at this, Alex. If it was just some random killing, you and your guests are in just as much danger as anybody in town." Alex tried to say something, but Armstrong held up his hands. "Slow down. I don't believe this is random for a second. What else have we got? Greed is always an awfully strong motive. I imagine Wellington's son could have a stake there. If he's the killer, there shouldn't be any further threat. Other reasons? How about sex, blackmail gone bad, hell, who knows, maybe he saw something he shouldn't have seen."

There was a hitch in the sheriff's words, and Alex said, "There's something you're not saying, isn't there?"

Armstrong stopped his search for a second to look at Alex carefully, then the sheriff admitted, "You could have a crazy killer on your hands who's just getting his first taste of blood. It doesn't feel right, though. I don't think anybody else is going to get killed."

"What if you're wrong? Is there anybody you can station out here until you figure out who killed Reg?"

"Alex, I wish to heaven I could, but with my budget, I can barely keep two cruisers on the road. What with Bobby James on vacation and all, I don't see how I can help you there." He slapped Alex on the shoulder. "But don't you worry now. I'm going to keep my eyes and ears on this place. We'll get this killer, you mark my words."

Alex shrugged. "Sheriff, I've got to tell my guests what's been happening. At least that way they'll have the option of leaving if they're not comfortable staying at the inn."

"I understand that. I just wish I could keep them all here. I know the killer could be long gone, but I can't help thinking he's still around."

Alex shrugged. "If you can keep them here on your own, fine, but they have a right to know what's going on."

Armstrong pulled at his chin and frowned as he kicked at the grass. "It's too bad we didn't find anything here."

They walked back out front and the sheriff got into his cruiser and drove away.

Alex peered up at the lighthouse, and for just a moment it felt as though the tower was looking back down at him. The structure had always been a comfort to him, but as an errant cloud scudded across the sun, the lighthouse was bathed in muted darkness; there was an almost sinister shadow enveloping it until the sun broke free again.

Alex prayed the killer was long gone from Hatteras West, but he had a sneaking suspicion that just wasn't the case.

He could only hope that there would be no more murders at Hatteras West.

6

"I finished the occupied rooms, Alex. Is there anything else you need done this evening?"

Alex looked up from his seat on the porch to see Elise standing directly in front of him. He'd forgotten all about her, and it took him a second to react.

She must have caught the vacant look in his eyes. "Funny, I thought I was more memorable than that."

"I'm sorry," Alex said as he sighed. "I've been sitting here since they took Reg's body away. I must be in some kind of funk. We were really close." He shook his head, then added, "I'm having a tough time with it."

A look of concern swept over her face. "I'm sorry you lost your friend." She added, "You'd probably prefer to be alone. If that's all for today, I'm going to go into town and get something to eat."

Alex realized that in his haste to hire Elise, they hadn't even discussed salary. He got up from his seat abruptly and said, "Why don't we go together? Dinner's on me. It'll give us a chance to talk, plus I can write the meal off on my taxes as a job interview."

"I don't see how you can interview me if I've already got the job." There was a sudden coolness to her words, and ordinarily Alex would have taken the rebuff in stride and moved on.

Instead, he said sternly, "I'm not making a pass, Elise; I've already got a girlfriend, but she's out of town on business and I just don't want to eat by myself tonight. You're certainly under no obligation to eat with me."

Elise's eyes softened. "I'm sorry, Alex, I overreacted. I guess I'm kind of defensive."

"Don't worry about it, it's not a problem," Alex said as he stayed in his chair.

Elise stood there a moment, then said gently, "If the dinner invitation is still open, I'd be happy to join you tonight."

Alex said with a slight smile, "Maybe you should buy, then. That way there won't be any doubt in your mind that it's not a date."

Elise laughed for the first time since Alex had met her. It was a rich throaty sound that instantly warmed the air between them. "I'll be glad to, if you'll pay me for today's work."

"Tell you what, I'll buy dinner tonight after all. We haven't even discussed your salary yet."

Alex considered their choices for dinner.

Elkton Falls had only two decent restaurants, Buck's Grill and Mamma Ravolini's. Buck's was basically a diner with booths and a front bar, while Mamma's as the townsfolk referred to the latter, was a sit-down restaurant run by an older woman named Irma Bean.

The closest Irma had ever been to Italy was watching a documentary on Public Television, but she believed the name Mamma Ravolini's sounded more appropriate for her pasta-oriented menu than Bean's Family Restaurant. Alex's girlfriend, Sandra, was always dragging him to Charlotte to try the Queen's City's latest and greatest, but Alex preferred the food in Elkton Falls.

Their choice was narrowed even more since Buck's only served breakfast and lunch. "How's Italian sound?"

Elise smiled. "Mamma Ravolini's it is. I've been in town two weeks, and I still haven't had a chance to eat there. The local branch of Dantons isn't schooled in the fine art of food preparation. They've been taking advantage of my background and keeping me in the kitchen since I arrived." Elise added, "If we've got hot water now I'd like to grab a shower before we go."

"According to my handyman, we should have plenty of hot water, so help yourself." He glanced at his watch and grinned. "But I thought you were starving."

Elise said, "If I'm not ready in fifteen minutes, you have my permission to go on without me."

Alex didn't believe her, but he figured he might as well use his time productively and pay some bills. He was writing the third check when Elsie joined him.

She was dressed in a floral print dress that fell just below her knees. Her hair had been brushed out and was pulled back away from her face. In short, she looked delightful.

He got up from his chair. "I think I'd better change, too. I'll be ready to go in a minute."

Elise said, "Nonsense. You look fine."

"Okay." They walked out to Alex's battered gray

Ford pickup after Alex posted a "Back After Supper" sign at the front desk. He winced slightly, wondering what Elise would think of his transportation. Gamely, he opened the passenger door and held it for her. Too late, Alex remembered that many modern woman considered gallant behavior offensive. But Elise smiled at the courtesy, and Alex had to hide his own grin in return. If his truck put her off, she didn't show it. She slid onto the vinyl seat as if she'd grown up riding around in a long-bed pickup.

As he drove down Point Road toward town, Alex asked, "What kind of background do you have that makes you such a fine cook? I can't imagine Mrs. Danton turning her kitchen over to just anyone."

"Don't kid yourself. She thought it was wonderful having someone else feed her clan. I didn't really mind, though. Cooking has always been a hobby of mine. I got my degree in hotel/motel management from West Virginia University, and I picked up some tips from a Marriott chef I worked with in Greensboro."

Alex looked over at his passenger. In the fading light of the day, he studied her face for a moment to see if she was pulling his leg. But she returned his glance with a steady look that told him she was telling the truth.

Alex laughed deeply. "I've hired someone to be my maid who has better qualifications to run my inn than I do! You must think I'm an idiot."

Elise said, "I think nothing of the sort. You didn't have time to ask, and it didn't seem important to tell you. I would have done just about anything to get out of that house anyway."

Alex heard Elise sigh heavily beside him. They drove in silence for a few moments. She finally broke the quiet. "I grew up in a little hotel in the West Virginia mountains. We had nine rooms and a restaurant. It wasn't much, but my folks and I were happy. I decided that someday I was going to run one of the big chains single-handedly, so I got my degree from WVU and headed out into the cold cruel world two years ago. I landed a job at Marriott and discovered that corporate life wasn't for me. There were too many forms, too much paper work, and not enough interaction with people. I was getting to the point where I wasn't even seeing the guests anymore, so I quit."

"And you ended up as a house guest of the Dantons? That's a pretty far fall."

Elise said softly, "I wouldn't say I was a guest; I was more like a cook and a maid. It didn't matter, though; I just needed some time away from everything. Now I'm so grateful to get out of that house I should be paying you for this job."

Alex coughed once. "Speaking of money, we're near the end of our season here, and things are a little—."

Elise cut him off gently. "Why don't we give each other a one-week trial? We'll see how it goes, and we can talk about money after that."

Alex nodded. "I'm willing to handle it that way if you are."

Mamma Ravolini's gravel parking lot was jammed, but Alex managed to slide the truck into a newly freed slot.

As they went inside, it took Alex's eyes a second to adjust to the dark interior. The only light came from thick red candles, one per table. The effect always gave Alex the impression that the dining room was on fire. The walls of the restaurant were lined with photographs of the near-famous who had dined at Mamma Ravolini's, each adorned with a hastily scrawled signature and good wishes. Alex had studied the pictures one evening. The most famous face he'd found belonged to a Charlotte newscaster who had been fired for filing false stories. Nevertheless, the picture had remained on the wall in its place of honor.

The aromas of pizza, lasagna and ravioli filled the air like a humid summer breeze. Alex loved the place, and Irma Bean's familiar openness, but he rarely made it into town during tourist season, and Sandra never wanted to eat at Mamma's even if he was free.

There was no one at the front, so Alex started looking for an empty table when he felt two arms embrace him. He looked down to see Irma herself giving him the bear hug of his life. She was a short thin woman who somehow managed to keep her slight figure around all the heavy sauces and rich desserts the restaurant served. Though Irma was a tiny woman, she had the longest reach Alex had ever seen, and the warmest heart, too.

"It's been too long since I've seen you, Alexander."

Alex said, "Hi, Irma. I'd like to introduce you to Elise Danton."

Irma released her grip on Alex and took Elise's hand in hers. "You're the girl who's been cooking for the Dantons? An hour ago they told me your veal picata was better than mine."

Elisa offered tentatively, "I'm sure your picata is marvelous."

"When it comes to cooking, I'm always willing to learn. So, are you going to share your secret with me?"

"Well, it's really all in the—"

Irma held up her hand and shushed Elise. "Not here,

I don't want everyone listening in. Let's go back to the kitchen, and you can tell me there."

Elise offered Alex a quick smile. "Excuse us, will you?" To Irma, she said, "I'm ready if you are. It's easier to show than explain, anyway."

Irma slapped Alex on the back. "I like this girl. Go find a table and eat some breadsticks. We'll be with you in a bit."

Alex made his way to an open table and sampled the homemade bread while he waited for Elise to finish up in the kitchen. He saw a few glances come his way, and he knew that if Sandra were in town, she would have heard about the dinner before they were finished with dessert. It was like that, living in a small town. Alex knew he would have to make a preemptive strike and tell Sandra about the business dinner first himself. Not that he had to justify his every action to her.

When Elise came back to the table, she let a slight grin slip out as Alex jumped up to grab her chair.

As she sat down in the offered seat, Elise said, "You really are quite the gentleman, aren't you?"

Alex said, "I've been trying to break the habit, but I'm not having much luck. To be honest with you, I'm sick of being lectured about what a modern woman will or will not put up with. I was raised to be polite to ladies and older folks. My mother wouldn't have any luck understanding the world today."

Elise caught and held his eye, and Alex felt the intensity of her look. In a serious tone, Elise said, "I think your manners are refreshing. Don't try to change them on my account."

"Thank God. It'll be wonderful just being myself."

Elise added, "Just don't treat me any differently than you did Marisa while we're at the inn, okay?"

Alex smiled slightly. "I kept a clean handkerchief available for her crying jags. Do I need to offer the same service to you?"

"No, but thanks for asking. Marisa is something else, isn't she?"

"That's one way of putting it." Alex opened his menu and studied the offerings. When he looked up, he noticed Elise was looking at him instead of the menu.

Alex said, "What's the matter, do I have bread crumbs on my face?"

"No, it's just that I took the liberty of ordering for us. Irma wanted to see how I prepared my picata, so I made three."

Alex smiled. "She's a hard woman to resist, isn't she? I've never been able to say no to her myself."

"I think she's delightful."

As if on cue, Irma came to their table carrying two steaming plates filled with all of his favorites. Irma knew what Alex liked, since he always ordered the same thing every time he came to the restaurant. He noticed that there was also a small portion of veal picata on his plate, along with the spaghetti and the ravioli combination platter he normally requested.

Irma surveyed the table. "What, no wine? You can't eat my food without a touch of the grape. I won't allow it." She called over her shoulder to their waiter, "Marty, bring a nice bottle of Chianti, on the house."

Elise took her plate from Irma. "So what do you think of my recipe?"

Irma gave out a hearty laugh. "It was delicious. I ate my own in the kitchen, and then helped myself to half of Alex's. You can come back anytime, Elise, with or without this fellow here."

Elise offered her thanks as Irma moved to another table across the room. Alex hadn't realized how hungry the day's activities had made him. He ate with hearty gusto and was surprised to look up from his empty plate to see Elise smiling at him.

She grinned and said, "So, how did you like the picata, or did you have a chance to taste it?"

"I missed lunch, and everything was so good." He kissed his fingertips in the air. "The picata was excellent."

Elise's dimples appeared. "It's nice to see someone enjoy a meal so much. The Dantons were much more critical eaters, even though they always managed to clean their plates."

Elise abruptly changed the subject. "I've been dying to ask you about this, but I really don't know how to go about it."

"Tonight, all answers are half-price, and the first one's free. Ask away."

"How on earth did your lighthouse get to be built in the mountains? And how did you end up owning it?"

"That's two questions, but I can satisfy your curiosity with one long, drawn-out story that will probably bore you to tears. It's all ancient family history."

Elise shifted her chair a little closer to Alex as she took another sip of wine. "I'd really love to hear about it."

Alex said, "It all started back in 1883. My great-grandfather Adlai Winston had a farm about forty miles from here in Alexander County. A fellow named J. O. Lackey found a vein of mica on the property next to

Adlai's. Lackey knew about precious stones and such, so he was bright enough to keep looking, since mica's one of the indicators that there's a chance of gemstones nearby. Turns out he found thirty-six small emeralds. Well, that got Adlai awfully curious, so he started scouting around on his own property. It soon became apparent he was sitting on a war chest full of emeralds and other precious stones. The biggest one he pulled out weighed in at just under thirteen carats."

Elisa interrupted. "Mercy. That must have been worth a fortune."

Alex smiled softly. "Yes, and that's what Adlai got for the stone. This was all before the federal income tax, too, so the money was all his to keep. After a while, the stones became more and more scarce. Adlai found a mining company headquartered out West interested in his property, so he sold out. It made him a wealthy man.

"Three months later, the mining company found the Panther Star."

Elise sat up in her chair. "That was found around here?"

Alex shook his head sadly. "On my family's land, only it didn't belong to them anymore. One thousand one hundred seventeen carats. It broke Adlai's heart when they found that stone. He couldn't bear to hear the jibes of his old neighbors and friends anymore, always laughing at him behind his back, calling him an old fool for selling out. So Adlai started looking for a change of scenery. Travel was difficult back then, but somehow he managed to end up at the Outer Banks on the North Carolina coast. That's when he fell in love with the lighthouse at Cape Hatteras."

Alex glanced at his watch and said, "We could continue this another time. It's getting late, and tomorrow is going to come awfully early."

Elise pleaded heartily. "You can't leave me hanging without the full story. I still don't know why the lighthouse was built here."

"Okay, you win." Alex asked, "Now where was I?"

Elise eagerly supplied the start-up point. "Adlai had just made it to the Hatteras Lighthouse."

"Well, it was love at first sight. Adlai saw that bright diagonal white stripe going up the black tower, and he became bewitched. They say he could be charming when it suited his purpose, and he must have laid it on thick with the lighthouse keeper. Adlai lived with the man and his family as an honored guest in the main keeper's quarters, regaling them with stories of distant mountains the keeper's family had never seen. In return, Adlai got free run of the lighthouse and the grounds. To have heard the way my grandfather told it, Adlai dearly loved the brick and stone of the lighthouse.

"Then he fell in love again, this time with a young woman. The principal keeper's daughter was just around marrying age, and the two of them started spending more and more time together. The keeper's concerns turned to delight when Adlai proposed marriage to his daughter Hannah, then his joy turned to sadness when the two announced that immediately after the wedding, they would be heading back here to the foothills."

Elise said, "That must have killed her, leaving her family, everything she knew and loved."

Alex smiled. "They were in love, and that was the way things were back then. Adlai missed his home, and Hannah was eager to explore the world. After the ceremony, Adlai brought his new bride back to the mountains he loved. Initially, he bought some property near the old farmstead, but he soon grew tired of his old neighbors and friends and decided he and Hannah should have a fresh start together. He looked around, and with Hannah's approval, they brought the land the inn is sitting on now."

Elisa leaned forward. "Tell me about the lighthouse."

Alex continued as if she hadn't spoken. "After four years of wedded bliss and three babies, Hannan nearly died delivering the last child. That was my grandfather Adam."

"Hey, do all the Winston boys have names that start with 'A'?"

"It's a tradition the family has kept for as long as anyone can remember. Anyway, Hannah loved Adlai, but she never got over losing the lighthouse, the ocean, and her family. Adlai understood how she felt. He was willing to take her back home for an extended visit to show her parents their new grandchildren as soon as the child she was carrying was born and old enough to travel. But it was no easy birth like the others had been. Hannah nearly died during the delivery, and the strain of the birthing left her too weak to travel, since the trip to the coast was an arduous journey back then. Hannah never got over her homesickness, and her health continued to fail. That's when Adlai got his idea. He'd build his wife a lighthouse of her very own. It wasn't the same as seeing her family and hearing the roaring crash of the waves again, but it was the best her husband could do with what he had.

"They say she thought he was crazy, but secretly delighted with the prospect of the construction. The original Hatteras lighthouse had been dedicated on her fourth birthday, December 16th, 1870. Adlai decided that Hannah's lighthouse would be finished by her twenty-fourth birthday. The original tower took eighteen months to build, but Hannah's took only fifteen months, once he managed to assemble a lot of the original construction crew."

Elise said, "How romantic of Adlai. Did Hannah love the lighthouse? I know, I bet it cured her, and she lived to enjoy being a grandmother herself. I can close my eyes and see her up on the observation deck now."

Alex shook his head sadly. "She died nine days before the tower was finished. It broke Adlai's heart to lose his wife. He shipped his children off to his sister for her to raise. They say that even the sight of those shining little faces that looked so much like their mother broke his heart all over again. For the rest of his life, the light was only lit one day in December every year, the anniversary of Hannah's birthday."

Alex glanced over to see Elise's eyes tear up. He nodded softly before continuing. "After Adlai died, my grandfather inherited the property. The family fortune was still viable then, but mismanagement of the trust Adlai had set up wiped out everything but the ownership of the lighthouse and the forty-odd acres I have now. By the time Dad took over, he was afraid he'd lose the lighthouse itself. That's when he decided to turn the place into an inn."

Elise dried her tears, then said, "If I'm going to work a full day tomorrow, we'd better get back to the inn. Alex, I had a lovely evening."

Alex stood up too. "I hope I didn't bore you with my family history."

Elise said softly, "Don't be silly. Thank you for sharing it with me. It makes Hatteras West feel like home to me."

7

Alex paid the bill, leaving a more generous tip then usual, and escorted Elise back to the truck.

The weather had changed during their time inside the restaurant. A heavy fog was starting to roll in, giving the air a moisture-laden density that he could almost taste. Though no rain was falling, they were still damp from the mist before they could reach the dry shelter of the truck interior.

In the darkness of the truck cab, Elise said, "We've been avoiding the topic all evening, but I think it's something we need to discuss before we get back to the inn. Alex, who do you think killed Reg Wellington?"

He kept his eyes on the billowing clouds of fog that blanketed the road as he went over his theories. "I suppose Junior is the prime suspect. He claims to have been asleep out on the loop trail when his father was murdered, but I have my doubts. I know from Reg, and by Junior's own admission today, that he stands to inherit just about everything his father had."

Elise said, "What do the police think?"

"I'm not sure about Armstrong. He hasn't even bothered to question anyone yet as far as I know, but Doc Drake seems to trust him, and I have to give him points for that. To be honest with you, before today I never had much cause to think about Calvin's competency one way or another."

He saw her nod solemnly in the dim light from the dashboard. "So that's why you're trying to come up with the answer on your own. Who else is on your suspect list?"

In his mind, Alex thought about who might have killed Reg before answering. "Joel Grandy got into a big argument with Reg last night over a chess game. I had to step in to keep the two of them from slugging it out. Is it enough reason to kill a man? Still, Junior and Joel seem to be the most obvious suspects so far."

After a moment of silence, Elise added, "But you've got more people on your list, don't you?"

How in the world could this woman read him so well after only spending a few hours with him? "I admit those are just my favorites so far. Coming in as long shots, we've got Sam Finster's mysterious client who's trying to buy the lighthouse. Maybe he thought a murder would shut the place down for good. It could be Barb Matthews. She hates men in general, and it wouldn't surprise me one bit if she started her campaign to rid the world of all of us."

"She's in room 6, isn't she?"

Alex nodded glumly. "Since the day before yesterday. I only had to shift her three times before she was happy this time. Why do you ask?"

"I was cleaning her room this afternoon, and I

stubbed my toe on something under her bed. She must have two dozen rocks hidden under there. I can't imagine why she bothers bringing those things to her room."

Alex laughed. "That's nothing. Last year, I had a pair of retired hairdressers from Florida who collected pine cones. The only problem was, they didn't take them with them when they left. At least I can use the rocks if she leaves them. But collecting stones doesn't surprise me as a hobby around here. Haven't you heard? We're on the border of Rockhound Heaven. The first gold rush in the United States started eighty-five miles from here down near Charlotte. Rubies, sapphires and emeralds have all been found as close as thirty miles from where the inn is standing."

Elise sat up straighter in her seat. "Do you think there's a chance any of those stones in her room are worth anything?"

Alex shook his head. "Not if she picked them up on her hikes around here. I don't think there's ever been anything of value found near here, but the lure of close riches keep the guests coming." Alex smiled. "My dad used to salt the place just before every tourist season when I was growing up."

"Salt it? What does that mean?"

Alex explained, "He'd go up to a small town a couple of hours from here called Little Switzerland and buy worthless pretty stones to throw out on the grounds of Hatteras West before the brunt of his guests arrived. Whenever a guest found one of his planted stones, Dad would ooh and ahhh. Mom made him stop it, though, because she thought it was dishonest. I still stumble across one now and then myself. I don't think Dad ever gave it up entirely. It got to be kind of a joke between us."

Elise nodded. "That explains the rocks and the other odd things I've found, but it doesn't help us with the murders. It sounds like anybody staying at the inn could have killed Reg."

"It's worse than that. A lot of the locals like to climb the lighthouse steps for exercise. It wouldn't be out of the question if one of them happened upon Reg and killed him in the lighthouse. I just wish I could come up with some kind of motive. Maybe he saw something he shouldn't have when he was up there looking around. I keep wondering if Reg spotted a pair of lovers from the observation deck, and somebody wanted to protect the secret enough to kill."

As they pulled into the parking lot, the lights in the two separate buildings glowed like wayward pockets of brightness through the thick fog, though the lighthouse itself was shrouded in darkness. For a single moment, Alex was tempted to fire up the Fresnel lens and show Elise how well the beacon worked, but the last thing he needed was problems with the Elkton Falls Town Council.

Alex was holding Elise's door open for her when a scream split the heavy veiled night air.

All Alex could think of was that this time he wouldn't be too late. The fact that he might be another victim himself never entered his mind. For some reason unknown to him, a killer was making Hatteras West his personal playground, and Alex was going to stop him, or die trying.

Elise held on to his arm as he tried to pull away. "What was that?"

"I don't know, but I'm going to find out." Alex freed himself from her grip and headed for the keeper's house at a dead run. It sounded like the scream had come from that direction, but in the heavy fog, it was difficult to tell for sure. He glanced back to see Elise close behind, and he paused to take her hand as they hurried through the misty night. He couldn't afford to lose her in the fog.

When they got to the main part of the inn, they found one of the guests, Elizabeth Halloway, shivering in the cold night air. She was a woman who looked otherworldly in the daytime because of her fine porcelain features, golden translucent hair and her marked preference for stark white gossamer-thin dresses. In the dark misty night, Alex almost mistook her for a ghost.

"Was that your scream, Miss Halloway?"

The young woman nodded furiously, but couldn't say a word. Alex waited as she composed herself, taking several gulps of air. Elizabeth Halloway had come to the inn last week, but Alex had yet to share more than ten words with her. She'd exceeded the length of her planned stay by two days, and Alex was frankly grateful for the business.

He'd noticed that the slim, ethereal blonde liked to take long walks in the woods surrounding the inn and that she was a very private person. She'd even requested on her arrival that no one enter her room during her stay. Marisa had been more than happy to oblige.

When she could finally speak, Miss Halloway's voice was cracked and full of fear. "I saw a ghost."

Alex tried to keep his tone light. "Surely in this fog everything looks ghostly. It might have been someone going for a late stroll, or even a billowing cloud of fog. Last year I saw a unicorn myself."

Instead of warming to Alex's humor, Miss Halloway turned on him with a fiery scorn in her eyes. "I said I saw a ghost, and that's exactly what I meant."

Elise stepped closer to her, and Alex admired her calm poise. "No one's doubting your word for a moment. Where did you see it?"

Miss Halloway pointed one long, slim finger at the lighthouse. "It was going up the steps. I saw a light flash by each window. Then, in a break in the fog, I saw a ghastly white face peering out of one of the windows. I shall never forget those haunted eyes."

Elise said, "My goodness, you're shivering. Why don't we go brew a pot of hot tea while Mr. Winston checks the lighthouse."

Miss Halloway nodded absently, her eyes still on the lighthouse as she headed for the lobby of the annex. Elise shot one backward glance at Alex as the two women walked off into the fog. He wasn't sure what Miss Halloway had really seen, but after the murder earlier in the day it was something he would have to investigate. The killer may have returned to the scene of the crime, perhaps in search of an incriminating piece of evidence left behind. Taking a heavy flashlight and a croquet mallet from the storage shed near the lighthouse's front steps, Alex hurried to the tower.

Sure enough, the normally locked door banged gently in the breeze. Had he locked the door after the ambulance attendants had removed Reg's body? For the life of him, Alex couldn't remember. For an instant, he considered calling Sheriff Armstrong to investigate the mysterious light, but Alex knew there wasn't enough time.

Pausing at the outer door, Alex peered through the gloom of the darkened interior of the lighthouse. As he entered the lower landing, he saw that there was indeed a dim light moving above him.

Someone was up there.

Alex shut off his own flashlight, hoping that whoever was at the top of the lighthouse had failed to see it. He quickly shoved the light into his back pocket and grasped the metal handrail, still clutching the mallet with his free hand. Alex silently inched his way up the steps, always keeping his eyes on the shifting beam of light above him.

He stopped at the eighth landing, wondering if he should continue up or go back for reinforcements, when the light started down the top stairs toward him! Hugging the wall beside the steps, Alex hoped that whoever was coming down would miss him with their light.

The beam caught him squarely in the face.

"Who is that? Lower your light." Alex's voice rang out with more confidence than he felt.

"What are you doing stumbling around in the dark? I almost shot you." He quickly recognized the voice as Sheriff Armstrong's.

Alex replied, "I could ask you what you're doing up here yourself."

Armstrong turned his light toward the rounded wall and away from their faces. The sheriff grinned. "I had a thought to check the lens itself for evidence. If Wellington saw someone heading toward him he didn't trust, I figured he might have stashed something in the lens housing. It's the only hiding place worth a hoot up there."

Alex was impressed. He hadn't thought to look around for a dying clue. "Did you have any luck?"

Armstrong shrugged. "Just a couple more of those rocks we found before."

Alex explained, "Reg probably picked them up on a walk across the grounds. They're everywhere."

Armstrong replied, "Maybe he was going to drop them off the top of the lighthouse."

"Reg had more sense than that."

Armstrong grinned eerily in the light. "Son, don't ever underestimate a man's capacity for foolishness."

Alex shrugged. "If you're done looking around tonight, why don't you come inside and get a cup of hot tea? Elise is brewing up a fresh pot for one of our guests." Alex chuckled softly to himself.

"What's so funny?"

"Miss Halloway is the reason I was checking out the lighthouse. She said she saw a ghost climbing the stairs."

Armstrong smiled. "I thought I saw someone through the fog. Should I sneak around back and tap on the window? That'll give her a good jolt."

"I'm losing enough guests as it is. Let's not add to the stampede."

The two men walked down the metal stairs, talking mainly about the fog. When they got to the lobby, Alex asked Armstrong to wait out on the porch while he explained to the ladies what had happened. Instead of being relieved, Miss Halloway looked more flustered than ever.

"A murder in the lighthouse? My God, why didn't you tell me? I'm not staying another night in this place!"

Elise kept her voice calm and soothing. "We're all

upset about it, but there's no sense in panicking. We don't even know if the murderer is still around."

Miss Halloway jumped from her chair, stormed down the hall and disappeared into her room. Alex retrieved the sheriff. "Looks like she'd rather see ghosts than hear about dead bodies."

Armstrong frowned. "I'm sorry I spooked your guest, Alex. I just had to get back up there before anybody had a chance to tamper with any possible evidence."

Alex patted the man on the shoulder. "Don't worry about it. She's right, you know. I should have already told everyone staying here about Reg's death. I'll take care of that first thing in the morning. I sure hope nothing else happens tonight."

Alex turned to Elise. "At the rate we're losing guests, we may have to shut down Hatteras West before this is all over. You might be out of job before you even get started."

Elise moved over to the teapot and poured cups for Alex, Armstrong and herself. She took a sip, then said, "I'm not ready to give up just yet. I've got a stubborn streak a mile wide."

Alex was relieved to hear that Elise was willing to stay.

The sheriff said, "Well, I'd better be moving along. I think I'll offer your guest a police escort out of here. She shouldn't be driving in this fog if she's not used to the roads. After the scare I gave her back there, it's the least I can do."

Alex smiled. "Thanks, Sheriff. From the look on her face, you shouldn't have long to wait."

True to Alex's prediction, ninety seconds later Elizabeth Halloway stomped down the hallway toward Alex and Elise. Alex decided to take the offensive. "The sheriff is waiting to make sure you get into town safely. Don't worry about the rest of your bill. We'll consider your last two nights as compliments of Hatteras West."

She looked flustered by Alex's generosity, and without uttering another word, Elizabeth Halloway flung the door open and stormed out into the foggy night, Armstrong close behind her.

Elise chided him gently after they were gone. "Shame on you, Alex. You stole that poor woman's thunder."

Alex grinned. "Thanks for your help. You really are good with people, you know that?"

"It's a part of being an innkeeper. Now if you'll excuse me, I'll say good night."

"Good night," he called out.

After she was gone, Alex went through his nightly routine of checking the inn to be sure that all was as it should be.

It was still hard to believe that Reg was dead.

8

By the time Alex woke up the next morning, the fog had burned off in the early morning sunshine; it looked like another beautiful day.

He found Elise mopping the front lobby as he came out of his room. Alex said, "Good morning. You're getting an early start, aren't you?"

Her smile was warm and genuine when she looked up from her work. "I'm just about finished. I like getting a jump on the day. Didn't Marisa ever clean this beautiful wooden floor?"

"If she did, I never caught her at it."

Elise stopped working and walked over to Alex. "What do you do about breakfast around here?"

Alex said, "There's a kitchenette tucked in the back of my room. I've got eggs, milk and cereal; you're welcome to whatever you want."

Elise took a few final passes with the mop, then said, "Lead me to it."

Alex was thankful he'd made his bed and straightened his room. It was probably silly, but he didn't want his new maid to think that he was a messy housekeeper.

Elise headed straight to the kitchen and started rummaging through his meager pantry.

Alex said, "Marisa and I usually ate in shifts so somebody could be at the front desk. That's where I'll be if you need me."

Elise brought her head out of the cabinet long enough to say, "Have you eaten yet?"

"You don't have to worry about me. I've been taking care of myself for a long time."

She said, "It's no trouble. Alex, it's as easy to make an omelet for two as it is for one."

"You convinced me. I need to have a conversation with one of our guests, then I'll be in need of a hearty meal."

Elise frowned slightly. "Is there anyone left who doesn't know about Reg's death?"

"The one I've been dreading telling the most: Barb Matthews. I can't imagine how she's going to take the news. You know, I'm starting to have second thoughts about anyone staying here right now. The more I think about it, the less I like the idea of any of my guests being in jeopardy just because I want to make a few dollars. I'm going to do my level best without actually throwing them out to see if anybody will consider leaving the inn, at least until the murder is solved." Alex excused himself and headed over to Barb Matthews's room. Before he could knock on the door, he heard Sheriff Armstrong calling his name out front.

Back in the lobby, Alex asked, "Don't you have any other crimes to investigate around here?"

Armstrong said, "Not like this one. I need to interview your guests this morning. Do you want me to interrogate them on my own, or would you like to come with me?"

Alex shuddered at the thought of imposing on his guests anymore, but he knew the sheriff was right. He only wondered why the man hadn't interviewed them yesterday.

Alex said, "If you don't mind, I'd like to be with you when you talk to my guests. By the way, did Miss Halloway get out of town all right?"

Armstrong grinned slightly. "You don't have to worry about her. I interviewed her last night over a piece of pie and a cup of coffee."

"Mixing business with pleasure, Sheriff?"

Armstrong shrugged as he said, "I figured it was the only way I could get her story. That's the official version, anyway."

Alex said, "We may as well get started. Anybody in particular you'd like to speak to first?"

The sheriff thought about it for a moment before replying. "The son, I think. He seems the most likely suspect to me. You're close to this, Alex. What do you think?"

Finally, the sheriff was asking his advice. "I believe Junior's an excellent place to start. Let me tell you what I found out yesterday."

Alex told the sheriff about Junior's alibi and the pristine state of his clothes as the two men walked to Junior's new room. Alex had moved the son promptly to a spot in the annex away from his father's old room. That left the main house empty at the moment, and Alex had a sudden twinge of regret for his steadily decreasing bank balance.

It took four knocks to bring Junior Wellington to the door. Junior had managed to throw on a robe, but Alex could see he was still dressed in a pair of heavy flannel pajamas.

"What can I do for you, Alex? I don't remember requesting a wake-up call."

Armstrong stepped around Alex and entered the room uninvited. "My name's Armstrong. I'm the sheriff for Canawba County. I'd like to discuss a few things with you about your father."

Junior suddenly looked wide awake. "Did you find out who killed him?"

"The investigation is ongoing."

After Alex stepped inside, Armstrong closed the door and leaned against it as if he were cutting off Junior's escape route.

The sheriff said, "Where were you yesterday afternoon between the hours of three and five?"

Junior pointed to Alex. "I already told him. I was hiking the loop trail all afternoon."

"And could I possibly see the clothes you were wearing on your little hike?"

Junior bristled at the suggestion. "Really, Sheriff, I don't see why it's any business of yours what I had on yesterday afternoon. What possible relevance could that have to my father's murder?"

"You don't have to cooperate, but I'll be glad to get a warrant and search your room anyway. Now, are you going to help me find your father's murderer, or are you going to get in my way?"

"Of course I want to find out who did it." Junior turned and started rummaging in a pile of clothes at the base of his closet. After picking out a pair of pants and matching shirt that looked somewhat familiar to Alex, he turned back to the two men.

Armstrong took the clothes and started examining them closely. Alex could see from his vantage point that the back of the pants and one cuff of the shirt had grass stains and smudges of dirt that he was sure hadn't been there the day before.

Alex stepped in. "Are you sure this is what you were wearing yesterday?"

"I know my own clothes."

Armstrong shot Alex a withering look before speaking to Junior again. "On this hike, did anyone happen to see you?"

"I think I'm beginning to see where you're going with this. Surely you don't think I murdered my own father?"

The sheriff puffed out his chest. "Don't act so surprised; it happens all the time. Why don't you humor me? I repeat, did anyone see you while you were out on the trail?"

"Besides a few squirrels and a couple of mockingbirds, no one. Wait a minute, that's not quite true. I happened upon a curious little woman scurrying along the path."

"Will she verify seeing you?"

Junior frowned. "I don't think so. She was so absorbed in her walk that she never looked my way. I was slightly embarrassed having been caught napping, so I remained silent while she passed me."

Armstrong said, "So you don't have an alibi. You're not planning to leave the inn any time soon, are you Mr. Wellington?"

Junior's back stiffened. "Not until my father's murderer is found."

Armstrong took the clothes Junior had claimed to have worn and started for the door.

"Where are you going with my things?"

"They're possible evidence, Mr. Wellington. You'll get them back after we've had a good look at them."

Armstrong and Alex walked out of the room. Once the door was closed, the sheriff started in on Alex. "Clean outfit? Do you *see* these grass stains?"

Alex protested, "I'm telling you, he either pulled out the wrong clothes or he added the stains later. That outfit was clean when I saw him in it yesterday."

Armstrong folded the clothes up, tucked them under his arm, then pointed to the next door. "Who's in here?"

"That's where the recently departed Miss Halloway was staying."

"Don't worry about her. I know where I can reach her if I need to. Who else is still staying at the inn?"

They moved to the next room across the hall. "The main quarters are empty, everyone's in the annex at the moment." Alex dreaded interrupting the occupant in room 6. He was sure Barb Matthews would not be pleased by the two men's questions.

There was no reply to their knocking.

Armstrong said, "Open it up anyway."

"Sheriff, my guests have a certain right to privacy in my inn."

Armstrong paused for thought. Abruptly, he said, "Did you hear that?"

"What? I didn't hear anything."

The sheriff said, "Alex, I could have sworn I heard someone cry out for help. Open the door."

Alex groaned softly as he opened the door with his pass key. His hands were shaking at the thought of catching the old woman coming out of the shower. She would probably sue him for his last dime, which was what he was just about down to.

The room was blessedly empty.

Alex whispered, "What are we looking for?"

Armstrong said, "We're not looking for anything. We were standing in the hallway and we thought we heard someone calling for help."

Alex had to agree that the logic would probably hold up if they were discovered in the room. "You do your search. I think I'll go get her some fresh towels."

Alex went down the hall and peeked his head into his own room. It looked like Elise was just finishing up her breakfast preparations.

Alex said, "That smells wonderful. What is it?"

"The Elise Danton Western Omelet. I hope you're hungry. I got carried away and made enough for three."

"That's good. We'll probably have to feed Sheriff Armstrong, too."

Alex quickly brought her up to date on what had happened. "Don't worry about Junior's clothes. When I clean his room, I'll snoop around a little. In the meantime, why don't you retrieve the sheriff and I'll set another place at the table."

Alex did just that, finding the sheriff closing the door to the Matthews woman's room as he entered the hallway. It was just as well. He'd forgotten to get fresh towels from the linen closet anyway.

Alex said, "Find anything?"

Armstrong jumped a foot in the air. "You've got to

quit sneaking up on people like that. It's going to get you in trouble one of these days."

Alex bit his lip to keep a smile from showing. "Was there anything in there worthwhile?"

"Nothing but a pile of rocks. Crazy, huh?"

Alex laughed. "Sheriff, I've yet to meet a 'normal' guest at this inn. We attract the unusual types. I had one guest who collected nothing but gravel because he thought the color was pretty. I've uncovered hordes of pinecones, branches, even old bottles. What surprises me is so many of the guests don't take their 'finds' with them. I could build a rock garden just with the stones I haul out of my guest rooms every season." The sheriff's stomach rumbled noticeably, and Alex asked, "Have you had your breakfast yet?"

Armstrong patted his big belly. "I had a quick meal, but I could always use another bite. What'd you have in mind?"

"Elise is fixing an omelet in my room, and she's made more than enough for you to join us."

Armstrong raised one eyebrow. "I'd be pleased to join you, if three's not a crowd."

Alex let a little of his ire enter his voice. "It's not a date, Armstrong, it's breakfast. Eat or not, suit yourself."

As the two of them walked toward Alex's room, the sheriff asked, "Is that what you two were doing last night at Mamma Ravolini's?"

"It was business," Alex said sternly. That was one of the problems with small towns. Everybody made it a point to know what everybody else was doing. Alex didn't dignify the question with any more of an explanation than that.

The smells coming out of his room were pure ambrosia to the bachelor chef, and quite out of the ordinary compared with his usual breakfast—a bowl of cold cereal.

One of the game tables in the lobby had been set up like it belonged in a fine restaurant. Elise had found a tablecloth in the linen closet and had even adorned the center of the small table with some wildflowers she found outside.

Elise said, "Why don't you two go ahead and sit down. I'll have everything ready in a minute."

As the three of them ate, they discussed everything but Reg's murder, though the unspoken topic hung over their thoughts like gravid black clouds.

Alex noticed that, though it was the sheriff's second breakfast, there was nothing left on the man's plate but a hazy shine.

For a second it looked like the sheriff was going to loosen his belt another notch. He leaned back in his chair instead and said, "Ma'am, that was the best omelet I've ever had. You ought to open up your own restaurant."

Elisa smiled slightly. "I believe I've found an appreciative audience at last."

"It really was delicious, Elise. Thank you," Alex added.

Armstrong pushed himself away from the small table and said, "I hate to eat and run, Elise, but I've got a murder to solve."

Alex watched as the sheriff got up and headed back toward the guest rooms. He lingered over his coffee until the sheriff asked pointedly, "Aren't you coming?"

Alex said, "To be honest with you, I've lost my taste for it. Do you really need me?"

"Your guests are bound to be a little more cooperative if they see the hotel owner with me. Besides, if they aren't in, I'd like a quick peek into their rooms. I can't do that without you and your key."

Alex reluctantly caught up with Armstrong as he headed toward the next occupied room. This one belonged to Emma Sturbridge.

9

Alex said, "I keep telling you, Sheriff, Mrs. Sturbridge just arrived last night. She can't possibly know anything about Reg's murder."

"Why don't we talk to her anyway? She may have seen something on her way in."

Alex knocked a final time before using his pass key to enter the room. There was no sign of the woman anywhere. As he had suspected, Emma Sturbridge kept her belongings neat and orderly. He could usually tell after meeting his guests for the first time what kind of tenants they'd be.

"Wonder where she's off to?"

Alex turned to the sheriff. "She's another rockhound. Where do you think?"

Armstrong let the gibe pass and pivoted out of the room. "Who's next on your list?"

"Joel Grandy."

"Is he another one of your harmless guests?"

Alex had to admit he wasn't sure, as he shared his

observation of the chess argument with the sheriff. Armstrong looked pleased. "Finally, another legitimate suspect. Unlock the door."

Alex ignored the sheriff and knocked loudly first. Grandy swung the door open before Alex had a chance to rap a second time.

"What can I do for you gentlemen? I was just getting ready to go into town."

Armstrong stepped deftly in front of Alex and took over the interview. "I'm investigating the murder of Reg Wellington. I understand the two of you had words the night before last about a chess game."

Grandy looked directly at Alex as he spoke. "I already explained the incident to my host."

Alex lifted his hands in apology to the man. He hated passing gossip on to Armstrong, but his friend had been murdered, and he was determined to find the killer. It was no time to be concerned with good manners.

Armstrong continued. "Why don't you go over it for me. Tell me why you two nearly came to blows."

Grandy stepped back from the doorway, and the other two men quickly followed him into the room. "My God, it was an innocent chess game. Surely you don't think I'd murder someone over a friendly match. I never laid a hand on him. Ask anybody."

"It didn't sound too friendly to me the way it was described."

Joel shrugged. "Tempers flared a little, but I didn't kill him. There's been enough death in my life lately without my adding to it. I don't know if you've heard, but I recently lost my wife to cancer."

Armstrong changed tacks. "Where were you between the hours of three and five yesterday afternoon?"

Grandy leaned into the sheriff. "Unless you're planning to arrest me, I'm through with you and your questions."

Armstrong replied, "You may be a material witness to a murder, so I'm formally requesting that you stay on site until I'm done with my preliminary investigation." Alex started to protest, but it was too late. Armstrong turned on his heel and started out of the room. Alex didn't know whether to follow or not, until the sheriff turned to him with a steely gaze. "Let's go."

Alex didn't like either man's bullying tone, but he wanted to stay close to Armstrong in case the sheriff learned anything new about the murder.

Once they were in the hallway, Alex asked, "Why did you give him such a hard time?"

Armstrong frowned. "I didn't like his attitude. People should have more respect for the law."

Alex was about to reply when Elise joined them. The second he saw her face, Alex knew that something was wrong.

"What's happened? You're as pale as a ghost."

"It's about Mrs. Sturbridge." Elise's voice was as weak as her complexion.

Armstrong stepped in front of Alex to get closer to Elise. "What happened? Don't tell me she's been murdered, too."

Elise shook her head, and Alex wondered what could shake her so. Elise, unlike her cousin Marisa, was a strong woman with a deep spirit.

He said, "Wait a second. Let me get you some water."

Alex hurried into the lobby and got a glass from behind the desk. He thought about adding some bourbon, but decided it was too early in the morning for that, even for medicinal purposes. Instead, he filled the glass with icy well water and offered it to Elise.

"Calm down, take a drink, then tell us what happened."

Elise took a healthy swallow of the cool water. When she spoke again, her voice was steady and solid, though more subdued than Alex was accustomed to.

"Mrs. Sturbridge was out on Bear Rocks. That's where she must have fallen. Mor Pendleton was hiking on his day off and found her at the base of one of the formations. He called an ambulance on his cellular phone and went with her to the hospital."

Bear Rocks was a part of Hatteras West's property, even though the formation was tied to the lighthouse area by the narrowest of trails. Alex wasn't surprised they hadn't heard the sirens. A dense copse of heavy hickory, oak and maple trees buffered the guest quarters, shielding them from even the most obvious sounds. Alex's father had cleared a parking area off the highway for townsfolk who wanted to hike or picnic at the site. It was more a public park than Winston land, though the property's deed was in Alex's name.

A related question came unbidden to Alex's mind. Why was Mor Pendleton out hiking in the first place? Alex knew the man's football injuries still nagged him with pain. He was the last person Alex would think would take up hiking as a hobby or a form of exercise. He'd have to ask his friend about that later. Right now, Alex had Mrs. Sturbridge's welfare on his mind.

Alex asked, "How bad is she?"

Elise patted his arm gently. "I'm sorry, the doctor said she's still unconscious, Alex. They just called from the hospital to tell us what happened."

Alex pulled away and headed for the front door as he called out over his shoulder to Elise. "I'm going to go see if there's anything I can do."

Elise caught up with him, and Alex noted that Armstrong was not far behind. She said, "Should I go with you, or stay at the inn?"

"I need you here." Alex grabbed his coat and turned to Armstrong. "Are you coming?"

The sheriff must have been feeling mulish, having his questioning sessions so harshly interrupted. "Why should I? The lady fell off some rocks. You'd better hope your insurance is paid in full. She'll probably sue the place right out from under you."

Though the family had opened the rocks to the guests of the inn and the townsfolk, there was no doubt that legally Alex *was* personally responsible for anything that happened on his land. Maybe he should have taken his brother's advice and deeded Bear Rocks to the county before anyone was injured on the property.

It was too late to worry about the liability now.

Alex snapped, "You don't think the two incidents could be related? Maybe Emma Sturbridge saw something, and someone was trying to make sure she didn't have the chance to tell us about it."

Armstrong snorted. "You're stretching, Alex. If I were you I'd take the lady some flowers and candy in case she comes out of it. As for me, I've got a murder to solve."

Alex kept his mouth shut and headed to his truck. In his rearview mirror, he spotted Elise waving good-bye.

As Alex drove to the hospital, he worried about his guest. He was hoping with all his heart that Emma Sturbridge was holding on. Alex honestly liked the woman, but that wasn't the main reason he desperately wanted her to revive. He had to believe her plunge and Reg's murder were related. At that moment, she held the best chance of identifying the killer, and her own assailant. It was only the faintest of hopes, but it was all Alex had.

Alex made his way through the halls of the hospital until he got to the intensive care unit nurse's station. Nearly out of breath, he said, "I'm here to see Emma Sturbridge."

A stern-looking young nurse glanced up from the chart in front of her and asked, "Are you a relative of the patient?"

Alex said, "No, but I'm the closest thing to a friend she's got around here."

The nurse's eyes softened. "I'm sorry. No one can go in but immediate family."

Alex asked, "Can you at least tell me how's she doing?"

"Wait here. I'll check."

In five minutes, the nurse came back. "Come with me. You can peek through the Intensive Care window, but that's as close as you can get."

Alex thanked the nurse and followed her into the hospital's restricted area. The smell of chemical cleaner permeated the air. Alex wondered for the thousandth time if the odious scent had any other function but to disguise the smells of death and dying.

They arrived at the Intensive Care Unit, and Alex peered through window at Emma Sturbridge. He had to take the staff at their word that it really was Emma. The hale and hearty woman Alex had met the night before was now enshrouded in hoses, cords and monitoring equipment. There was barely enough of her showing to make a proper identification.

A pretty young nurse working inside spotted Alex and came out. "Hi. I understand you were asking about Mrs. Sturbridge. Do you know her very well?"

Alex shook his head. "She's staying at my inn, Hatteras West."

The nurse smiled softly. "I'm Theresa DeAngelis. I just moved to Elkton Falls, but I've already heard all about your place. It sounds charming."

"Thanks." Alex gestured toward Emma. "How's she doing?"

Theresa stopped to consider the question. "Between us, it's too soon to tell. The doctor can probably tell you more, but he's on rounds right now."

Alex asked, "Did she manage to say anything when they brought her in?"

Theresa shook her head. "She hasn't so much as quivered a finger since she's been here. I don't know if anyone's told you, but she's in a coma."

Alex asked, "If she comes out of it, even for just a moment, would you have someone call me at the inn?"

Theresa's smile was filled with compassion. "I'll make sure somebody lets you know, even if she wakes up on a different shift."

Alex said, “I’d really appreciate that.”

The nurse nodded, and Alex added his good-bye and left without turning back. The sights and smells of the hospital were making him nauseous. Suddenly, the only thing Alex needed was fresh air. He stumbled out a nearby exit into the bright, autumn day and leaned against the coarse stone of the building’s exterior wall. The stone was warm on the back of his neck from the sunlight, and the smell of marigolds in a nearby flowerbed helped him forget the noxious odor of that corridor. It was hard for Alex to believe that the robust woman he had joked with the night before was fighting for her life on the other side of the wall.

10

Since Alex was already in town, he decided to pay a visit to Mor or Les's fix-it shop. He had a few questions for his old friend. Mor Pendleton was perched on his stool behind a long wooden workbench. The top was currently covered with the inner workings of an ancient cash register. The walls of the shop were filled with shelves, housing everything from a discarded vacuum cleaner chassis to a dismantled hand pump that Alex recognized as being the same kind that was used at the inn when he was growing up. There were magazines everywhere, from *Soldier of Fortune* to *This Old House.* Alex knew Mor's partner, Les, was a junkie for a particular form of the printed word, and he subscribed to just about every magazine he could get his hands on. Schoolkids doing fundraisers absolutely loved the crusty old man.

Mor was so deep in thought, tinkering with the register's bulky pieces, that he failed to hear Alex came in.

Alex picked up a piece of the register and said, "Looks like this one's down for the count."

Mor grinned at Alex. "These old printwheels are the dickens to fix, and to top it off, I can't get parts anymore. I've been robbing old machines to keep a few of them running, but there aren't that many left to vandalize."

"Why don't you tell the owner to give up and come into the electronic age?"

Mor's smile widened. "In the first place, that would lose us business. In the second place, this particular register happens to belong to Irma Bean. We swap repair work for free meals, and Les and I are both too set in our ways to take up cooking on a full-time basis."

Alex nodded absently and laid the part back down on the workbench. "I hear you found one of my guests at Bear Rocks today."

Mor nodded solemnly. "She was in pretty bad shape. Have you heard how she's doing?"

"I just saw her at the hospital. She doesn't look good." Alex picked up a large bright cog with a few specks of grease on it and twirled it in his fingers. "When did you take up hiking?"

Mor looked down at the printer again and removed another part. "There's the problem. I sure hope I can scrape up another paper-advancing gear. What did you say?"

Alex laid the cog back down on top of the workbench and asked, "When did you start hiking?"

As Mor worked, he explained, "A specialist in Charlotte told me it would be good for my knees to start walking some. I didn't want to go around town, so I figured you wouldn't mind if I worked out on your loop trail."

Alex said, "It's always open to you, you know that. When did you start? I'm surprised I haven't seen you around before."

Mor turned a slight shade of red. "I saw the doctor last month, but today was the first chance I had to get out and exercise. Don't tell on me, okay?"

Alex smiled. "Your secret's safe with me. Well, I'd better be getting back."

He started to leave when Mor called out, "You're not done here, fella."

"What's up?"

Mor's devilish smile came back. "I hear you got considerably farther with Miss Danton last night than I ever managed to. What's your secret, Alex? I thought you and Sandra were an item."

"She's out of town and I just wanted some company last night. My God, can't I change my underwear in this town without everybody knowing what color it is?"

"Buddy, you're the talk of the town. Every single man in Elkton Falls has asked that girl out, and you're the first one she's even smiled at. Irma told me all about it when I picked the register up this morning. When's Sandra due back in town?"

"She's coming in this afternoon. Elise Danton is a sweet girl and a pleasure to be around, but I've already got a girlfriend." Alex turned and had his hand on the door when he heard Mor choking.

He turned back in alarm, only to find the huge fix-it man doubled over in a badly controlled laughing fit.

Alex said, "Okay, so maybe I'm a little touchy, but she really is a nice girl."

Mor managed to stop his humor jag. "Irma thinks so, too. She wants to adopt her. Listen, I didn't mean to hit a nerve, I'm sorry. You've had a lot happen lately, haven't you?"

"More than I even want to think about."

Alex walked out of the shop feeling better, but that soon turned to dust when he spotted Sam Finster getting out of his Jeep Cherokee. Alex tried to duck back into the repair shop, but the eagle-eyed little weasel caught him before he could get inside.

"Alex Winston, just the man I want to see. You've saved me a trip out to the lighthouse."

Alex fought the urge to run. "Finster, I'm not selling. I told you, it's final."

Sam Finster missed Alex's cutting tone, or more likely chose to ignore it. "Since you've saved me the gas, at least let me buy you a cup of coffee and a doughnut."

Alex shook his head. "You go ahead, don't let me stop you. I was just on my way back out to the inn."

Finster smiled, his canines gleaming in the sunlight. "Now Alex, surely you have time for an old friend. Especially in your time of need."

Of course, with Finster's connections, he probably knew more about the murder and Emma Sturbridge's fall than Alex did himself. If he didn't go with the realtor now, he'd be hounded by the little ferret until he agreed to hear him out.

"I've got ten minutes to spare. Let's get this over with." Alex had found early on that no matter how rude he was to Sam Finster, the realtor still acted as if the two of them were the best of friends. Finster was the only person on the planet Alex was patently discourteous to, but then the rest of the town acted the same way toward him too. Finster had a way of bringing out the worst in people. For a fleeting moment, Alex wished if anyone had to take that fall from Bear Rock, it should have been the real estate man, then he quickly chided himself for wishing bad on anyone, even Sam Finster.

They walked over to Buck's Grill and found the owner's daughter Sally Anne waiting tables. Sally Anne could always be counted on for her bright, sunny smile.

In the hours between breakfast and lunch, the restaurant was oddly deserted.

Alex had heard from Buck that Sally Anne had decided to postpone college a year in order to save more money, but local gossip had it that she was more interested in seeing which college offered a scholarship to the town's local football hero, and incidentally, her boyfriend.

Alex asked, "How's Eric doing this season?" as he walked in.

Sally Anne's smile brightened even more. "He's on his way to breaking all the old school records. You should come out and watch him play sometime."

"I'd like that." He glanced at the menu board on the wall behind her. "Let me see, I'll have two of your freshest glazed doughnuts and a glass of chocolate milk. Finster's buying."

Her smile shifted to a grim crease as she turned to Finster. The real estate man winked broadly and said, "I'll have the same, honey." He turned to Alex. "You grab a booth, will you? I've got to make a quick call. Time is money, you know what I mean, sport?" His hacking laughter followed him all the way to the pay telephone outside the diner. The realtor was too cheap to invest in a cellular telephone even as the world around him went wireless.

Sally Anne delivered the two milks and the doughnuts before Finster had a chance to come back from the pay phone.

Alex said, "You don't like him much, do you?"

An uncharacteristic fury crossed the girl's face. "Every time he's in here he tries to pinch my bottom or find an excuse to brush against me. The man makes my skin crawl."

"You shouldn't have to put up with that. Why don't you tell Eric or your father?"

She grimaced. "Are you kidding? Eric would get thrown off the team if he got caught beating Finster up, and Daddy would kill the little sleaze."

She had a point. Her father, Buck Wilson, had been a state Golden Gloves champ, knocking down every opponent he met. Clippings on one wall chronicled his climb to the regional finals, where he had the misfortune to meet a future contender for the heavyweight championship title of the world. Buck's nose still bore the bend that Bomber Maxwell had put in it. He wore the crooked nose with pride, regaling every new customer with his blow-by-blow account of the fight. At fifty, Buck still looked like he could go ten rounds with any up-and-comer.

Alex suddenly thought of something. "Is your dad back in the kitchen now?"

"No, he's off on his morning jog, ten miles, rain or shine."

"Chances are Finster doesn't know that. Here's what you should do." Alex whispered his instructions to Sally Anne, whose grin grew wider with the telling.

Finster came back just as the two of them finished their discussion. Sally Anne managed to dodge Finster's groping paws; the realtor chuckled as he sat down.

Finster smiled and said, "What are you trying to do, Alex, go after every eligible woman in town? Leave a few for the rest of us, will you?"

Alex jammed a doughnut in his mouth to keep from saying something he might regret. Sally Anne made the doughnuts fresh every morning, and Alex loved the smell of the batter frying almost as much as the tender, moist taste of the pastries themselves. He ate both doughnuts, drank the milk, then glanced at his watch. "You've got two minutes, starting now."

Finster wolfed down the last bite of his doughnut. To Alex's disappointment, the man didn't choke. "My buyer has upped the offer for the inn. Why don't you grab it before my client finds out about what happened at Bear Rocks? You might avoid a lawsuit that way."

"Finster, I'm not going to sell the place unless the creditors are knocking down the door."

Finster's smile became predatory. "You think guests will flock to the Murder Inn next season? Come on, Alex, wise up and sell the white elephant while you can still get a good penny for it."

Alex had given that very option a great deal of consideration lately, but the Winstons had a stubborn streak, and Alex had inherited more than his share in the bargain. The nagging thought that a sale would no doubt give Finster a whopping commission steeled his resolve not to give the lighthouse up.

Getting up from the booth, he said, "Tell your buyer no sale." Alex nodded softly to Sally Anne, who was standing just inside the kitchen. According to his plan, the door was propped open, but Sally blocked the view. When she began speaking, it was loud enough for the two men to hear.

"I'm telling you, Dad, he tries to grope me all the time. I'm not waiting on him anymore. If you want his money, you serve him. I'm tired of him pinching my butt."

There was a pause, and Alex looked over at Finster. The man's face was completely white. Everyone in town knew that it took a lot to anger Buck, but one sure sign you had managed it was when he lowered his voice to a deadly whisper. The fact that Sally's pleas were going without response wasn't lost on Finster.

They heard Sally Anne's voice again, this time with a heartfelt plea in it. "Please don't get so angry, Daddy." If he so much as looks at me again, I'll tell you, I promise. Give Mr. Finster one more chance. You'd have an awful time explaining it to the jury, what with your temper and all."

Finster didn't wait around for a response. He mumbled something to Alex, then threw a twenty- dollar bill down on the counter as he raced for the door. As the weasel scurried down the sidewalk, Alex burst into a laughing fit.

Sally Anne joined him at the window as Finster sped away in his Cherokee.

She threw her arms around Alex. "I swear, I could kiss you for getting that leach off my tail." Sally Anne did just that, sliding into Alex's arms and planting a happy kiss on his cheek.

The sight of Finster's twenty on the counter brought the laughter back into her voice. "Looks like the movies are on me tonight. I hope Eric can skip curfew. You know Coach, he doesn't like his boys hanging out with the girls."

Alex grinned. "If Eric has any spunk at all, he won't let Coach's rules stop him. I know I wouldn't."

"How sweet of you. Tell you what, any time you get the craving for doughnuts, come on by. Your money's no good here as long as I'm waitressing."

Alex offered his thanks, then added, "If Finster ever does try to grab you again, you really should tell your father."

Sally Anne laughed. "You saw him run. I think he got the message."

When Alex got back to the inn, he was surprised to see Elise standing on the front porch of the annex. It was almost as if she were waiting for him.

He just hoped she didn't have any more bad news. He wasn't all that sure he could take it.

11

As he got closer, it appeared that Alex had worried for nothing. Elise looked happy to see him, until he made it to the front porch.

She frowned a moment, then said, "I see Sandra made it safely back to town."

"Not that I know of. Why do you say that?"

Elise gingerly pulled an ironed white linen handkerchief out of the front pocket of her blue jeans and dabbed the edge of it with her tongue. Alex felt sheepish as she rubbed at his cheek vigorously, displaying the unmistakable hint of lipstick now on the cloth.

Elise said, "It looks like *some* woman was trying to mark her territory with glossy red lipstick."

He stammered. "There's really a very simple explanation how that lipstick got on my cheek."

Elise suddenly turned away. "It's none of my business. Save your breath, Alex."

Alex was still trying to explain what had happened when Sheriff Armstrong's patrol car pulled up in front of the inn. There was another man in uniform with the sheriff, and from the look of his outfit, he worked for the state police. Alex thought now maybe somebody would believe him when he suggested that Reg's murder and Emma's fall were somehow related. He only hoped the two men's presence didn't signal another murder.

Armstrong ignored Elise, an officious look on his face. "Alex, I've got someone here I'd like you to meet."

When the state policeman joined them, Alex introduced Elise, then himself, as he offered his right hand to the patrolman.

The state policeman took it in a grip as firm as Alex's. The fellow, somewhere in his mid-twenties, sported a blond fuzzy crewcut and crystal blue eyes. His uniform looked freshly pressed, and Alex was nearly blinded by the shine on the officer's shoes. He was a large powerful man, almost too handsome, but the officer's open sincere smile made Alex feel at ease until he offered a tip of his hat to Elise. There was no doubt about it; Alex was startled to find that he was jealous.

The officer said, "I'm Sergeant Hicking with the State Bureau of Investigation. I understand you've had some activity out here in the past few days."

Alex offered a deep frown. "A bit too much for me. I'm glad the sheriff called for some help."

Armstrong stepped up and said, "It's my prerogative to call for assistance whenever I feel it's warranted. I asked the SBI to send somebody over to give me an opinion or two about the Wellington case."

The SBI officer said, "We function as an advisory

agency. Sometimes another set of eyes can see something in an investigation that others may have overlooked."

From the look on Armstrong's face, Alex knew the sheriff must have had mixed emotions about calling in the SBI. The sheriff had to be concerned that even if the case was solved now, his opponent in the election would claim Armstrong couldn't have done it alone. That didn't matter one bit to Alex. Solving Reg's murder was all that counted, and Armstrong's stock went up with Alex the moment he had called for reinforcements.

Alex asked, "So do you agree the two incidents are connected?"

Hicking's eyes perked up like a hawk spying fresh prey. "There's been another murder?"

Armstrong waved off Alex's words. "No, sir. Mr. Winston has the firm belief that one of his other guests was pushed off a rock this morning."

Elise surprised Alex when she stepped in. "I believe it too, Sheriff. Emma Sturbridge looked to be as surefooted as a mountain goat. I can't imagine her falling."

That got Hicking's attention back to Elise, just where Alex didn't want it.

"Are you a guest here, or are you Mr. Winston's girlfriend, by any chance?"

Alex saw Elise frown at the suggestion. "I work here. I'm the maid."

Hicking trotted out that huge grin again and offered Elise his hand. "That's hard for me to believe, Ma'am. Someone as pretty as you shouldn't be scrubbing floors."

Elise coolly withdrew her hand from the policeman's, and Alex saw her features frosting over. "What I look like has nothing to do with who I am, Sergeant. The work is honest, and it needs to be done."

Hicking realized he'd taken a misstep, but he didn't quite know how to atone for it. Suddenly all business again, he turned to Alex. "If you've got the key to the lighthouse, I'd like to see the murder scene."

"Oh, it's not locked. The sheriff let me reopen the lighthouse after his cousin came by."

Armstrong started blustering. "Come on, Alex, you know Irene's more than family. She's taken all the required classes. I didn't release the crime scene until she went over everything with her kit. We've got photographs and everything else we need down at the station."

Hicking said, "Settle down, Sheriff, nobody's saying your technician isn't fully competent. I'd like to see her after we leave here. Now, do you mind showing me where the body was found?"

Armstrong led the state policeman to the lighthouse door while Alex and Elise headed for the front porch of the inn.

Hicking stopped. "Aren't you two coming with us?"

Alex shook his head. "We've got an inn to run. If you need us, we'll be around."

Hicking headed up the lighthouse's front steps without another word.

Alex glanced over at Elise and found her staring thoughtfully after the state policeman.

With a great deal less calm than he felt, Alex said, "I still want to explain about the lipstick."

"It's none of my business, Alex."

He said, "I don't want you thinking I'm some kind of Romeo. I helped a waitress in town get rid of a problem, and she kissed my cheek in thanks. There was nothing else to it."

Elise said, "It's perfectly fine with me, Alex."

Did she believe him? Suddenly, it was very important to Alex that she did.

He said, "Hicking's a good-looking man, isn't he?"

Elise shook her head. "I suppose so, if you like that type. His attitude towards women needs a little work, if you ask me."

Alex laughed. "You gave him something to think about. Be nice, Elise. I know you can't help it, but you *are* attractive." Alex thought she was the most beautiful woman he'd ever seen in his life, but he kept that to himself.

As the two of them walked up the porch steps, Elise answered with a slightly vexed tone in her voice. "I had no control over what you see on the outside. I picked the right parents, that's all. People should care a little more about what's on the inside."

And that closed the discussion.

Alex went to the desk and looked at the work schedule Elise had drawn up. He saw that she had checked off each room on her morning rounds. As far as he could remember, Marisa had never made it all the way through the rooms in the course of a single working day.

When Elise returned to the front, Alex said, "I've got to work on the books. If you want to get started on the lobby floor, it needs a coat of wax desperately." He smiled, then added, "If you hadn't done such a good job mopping it, I never would have noticed."

They walked over to the storage closet and retrieved the buffer and wax.

Elise looked through the closet. "How about a couple of 'Slippery Floor' signs?"

"I never thought of that. Guess we'll have to pick some up."

"I swear, Alex. This place is a lawsuit waiting to happen. Have you ever had any trouble before from any of your guests?"

"Besides them stealing towels? None that I can think of. People didn't used to be so lawsuit happy. It makes me wish for the good old days."

Elise frowned. "No electricity, no indoor plumbing and no penicillin? No thank you. I'll keep the modern conveniences."

Alex said, "I guess you're right. I'm not even going to ask you if you need any help."

"That's a wise decision. I've handled a lot worse than this. My dad said I was the best worker he ever had at his hotel, and he wasn't just saying that."

"Wonderful. When you're done in here, you can rebuild the boiler."

Elise started rolling up the lobby's rugs, and Alex naturally joined in. "I took a peek at your heating and cooling system. I can't believe it's still running."

"That's what Mor keeps telling me. Give me a hand with this sofa, will you?"

Elise motioned to a large armoire that took up one corner of the lobby. "That piece is beautiful."

"You're not planning on moving it, too, are you?"

Elise said, "No, I can work around it. But the craftsmanship is wonderful."

Alex let a little pride slip into his voice. "Thanks. I helped my dad build it when I was fifteen."

"I'm impressed. There's certainly more to you than meets the eye, Alex."

"I'd like to think so."

In a few minutes, they had everything ready for Elise to begin.

Alex planned to work at his desk and started to wade through his financial records when Sergeant Hicking and the sheriff walked in.

Alex asked, "Have any luck?"

Armstrong started to say something when the state policeman shook his head. "We're not answering questions, Mr. Winston, we're asking them."

Alex persisted despite the obvious rebuff. "Do you know yet if the autopsy revealed anything unusual?"

Hicking looked at Alex closely. "Now why would you care about that?"

The question was blunt, so Alex made his answer match. "Reg Wellington was not just another guest to me. I've known him all my life, and counted him as one of my best friends in the world. I want to know who killed him, even if I have to step on a few toes to find out."

"Just make sure they're not the wrong toes. Okay, I don't see what it can hurt by telling you. The report said the wound was similar to one an ice pick would make."

Alex asked, "So what happens now?"

Hicking glanced down at his watch. "I've got a little time. Why don't you show me the spot where your other guest fell."

Armstrong said, "It's a waste of time. It was an accident, pure and simple."

Hicking's stare at Armstrong wilted the man. "It's my time to waste, and I'd like to see it. Do you have some urgent business elsewhere, Sheriff?"

"Nothing as important as this."

Hicking leaned near Armstrong and lowered his voice, though Alex was still able to make out the SBI man's words. "Find something."

Armstrong nodded. "On second thought, I think I'll stay here and monitor the radio."

Alex remained silent as he and Hicking walked down the path toward the rocks. Having the SBI man on the premises made Alex suddenly feel an odd loyalty to the sheriff. Elkton Falls was all the family Alex really had besides a brother he hardly ever saw, and while Alex himself had questioned Armstrong's competence on several occasions, he wasn't sure how he felt about an outsider coming in.

As the two men walked, Hicking said, "Is Miss Danton seeing anyone special right now?"

Alex felt the hair bristle on the back of his neck. So that's why the patrolman had wanted a few moments alone with Alex. He wanted to ask about Elise.

Stiffly, Alex replied, "I understand she's engaged, but it's really none of my business."

Hicking accepted Alex's statement. "I figured she was too pretty to be free." After a moment, he added, "Where are these rocks, anyway?"

"They're just up around the bend."

As Alex and Hicking turned the corner through a stand of thick trees, they got their first glimpse of Bear Rocks.

The rock formation was solid granite, worn away by the elements until the area was nothing but two acres of intriguing gray stone shapes. The formation was pocketed with holes and slides worn into the rocks, making it a spectacular playground for the young and agile. Alex had grown up on the rocks, dodging in and out of formations like a mountain goat. The stones became Indian forts, tree houses and deserted islands for Alex. He looked at the formations as a set of good friends, each one having its own shape and personality.

The state trooper whistled under his breath. "My God, it's no wonder someone fell off one of these stones. It's a miracle she didn't kill herself doing it."

Alex turned to Hicking. "Emma Sturbridge is a seasoned rockhound. She's used to terrain a great deal rougher than this. I can't imagine her falling."

Hicking turned away and headed back down the path toward the inn. "Unless you turn up a witness or Mrs. Sturbridge wakes up, I've seen enough. It was an accident, Mr. Winston, nothing more. Take my advice, don't borrow trouble."

Alex walked silently with the patrolmen back to the waiting cruiser. He still couldn't believe Emma could have fallen from the rocks, but he was getting tired of trying to convince everyone else.

They had just cleared the path when Alex heard a car horn. He spotted Armstrong leaning inside the cruiser with his hand on the center of the steering wheel.

Armstrong said, "Sorry to interrupt, but there's an accident out on Highway 321. I've got to handle it."

Hicking merely nodded. He offered his hand to Alex. "I'm sorry I can't stay, but we're overwhelmed with work due to the department budget cuts. The sheriff will let you know if we find out anything else."

Hicking moved around to the patrol car's passenger

side and got in. As the two law officers drove away, Alex realized that he'd received all the cooperation he was going to get out of the police. It looked like he was going to have to find Reg Worthington's killer himself. Why did everyone choose to discount Emma's fall as accidental? Sure, Bear Rocks could be treacherous at times, especially during a rainstorm, but the rocks had been dry when Emma had fallen. What could she have seen or known that would have been worth killing her for? It just didn't make any sense, and Alex couldn't begin to hazard a guess without more information.

He only hoped no one else got hurt before the murderer could be caught.

12

Alex started to walk back into the annex, but found the door locked. A few sharp raps on the frame brought Elise to the front.

As she freed the bolt, Elise said, "Take off your shoes. I hope your socks are clean, because the floor's not completely dry yet."

Alex smiled. "You sound just like my mother."

He slipped off his shoes and walked into the lobby. A quick inspection of the floor showed it to be in the best shape Alex had ever seen it. Alex asked, "Have you seen Junior Wellington today?"

Elise nodded. "He came by when I was working on the floor. He wanted to know something about the gem hunting around here."

"What did you tell him?"

"I've never been myself, but I gave him one of the brochures from Emerald Valley Mining Company I found behind the desk. Is that all right?"

"That's fine." So Junior was going to do a little

prospecting. Alex wondered if he was trying to learn a little gem identification on his own, and how it could relate to his father's murder. It seemed an odd way to pass the time if the man was indeed in mourning. There were several suspects in Alex's mind, but none ranked higher than Reg's own son.

"Elise, you've been working hard. How would you like to take tomorrow morning off and do a little prospecting with me? You should learn something about local gemstone mining."

Elise was quick on the uptake. "And if we happen to see Junior there, we can watch him and see what he's up to, is that it?"

Alex stammered a little at her having seen through him so quickly. "I didn't mean it as any kind of insult. I just thought—."

Elise interrupted. "It's honorable that you're trying to find out who murdered your friend. I'd be happy to go with you tomorrow, but what about our guests? Shouldn't someone stay here for them?"

Alex took quiet pleasure in the way she said 'our.' "The way I see it, one is dead and another is in a coma. That leaves one angry man and one sour old woman. We'll be following another guest around, so that's the whole lot of them since Miss Ethereal left us. I think we'll be fine."

Elise tried again. "Then what happens if the sheriff or that SBI man wants to talk to you about something?"

Alex offered a smile. "Then they can go rockhounding with us," he said, as he heard a car approach. Alex glanced out the window and saw Sandra's silver BMW, and from the expression on her face, he knew she'd already heard about Elise.

Sandra was still in the stylish gray suit she must have traveled in. Her short blonde hair was perfect, as always, and her skirt was just high enough to draw attention.

She smiled broadly at Alex, but when her gaze took in Elise, there wasn't much warmth in it.

She hugged Alex at the front door and made a show of kissing him.

"Did you miss me?" she asked.

Elise started to step away when Alex broke free. "Sandra, I'd like you to meet my new maid. Sandra Beckett, this is Elise Danton. Elise, this is Sandra."

Sandra took Elise's hand as she looked her over and said, "It's hard to believe you are part of the Danton clan."

Elise said quietly, "It's nice to meet you. Now if you'll excuse me . . ."

Sandra said, "Nonsense. I came to take Alex out to dinner. You simply must join us."

"Thank you, but I've already made plans."

Before Alex could say a word, Elise was gone.

Sandra said sharply, "I can't believe she's living here with you."

"She's my maid, Sandra. That's all. By the way, I'm fine, thanks for asking."

Sandra must have seen the storm clouds in his eyes. "I'm sorry. Alex, I just don't want to see you taken advantage of. The poor thing doesn't look like she'd be much of a maid."

"She's the best worker I've ever had at Hatteras West, Sandra."

She waved a hand in the air, dismissing his comment. "I'm sure she is. Now why don't you put on your best suit, and we'll go someplace nice to celebrate my homecoming."

"I don't feel much like going out tonight, Sandra. A lot has happened since you've been gone."

She arched one eyebrow. "I can see that. That's why we need to go out. You can bring me up to date." Alex started to protest, but Sandra wouldn't allow it. "You can be ready in ten minutes, Alex. Why stand here arguing?"

He said abruptly, "You know what? I don't seem to have much of an appetite. Go on without me."

Sandra looked stunned by Alex's refusal. "Maybe I'll do just that."

"That's fine by me," Alex said, instead of acquiescing like he knew Sandra was expecting him to.

Rebounding quickly, Sandra said, "On second thought, I am rather tired from my trip. Why don't we do lunch tomorrow instead, Alex?" She kissed him lightly on the cheek, then quickly drove away. Alex had to admire Sandra for one thing; she always knew when to cut her losses.

Suddenly, Alex realized that he'd just lost the chance to have dinner with two different women.

Tonight, he'd be eating alone.

Elise came out just as Alex was lighting the night's fire.

"I thought you two went out," she said.

"Sandra suddenly decided she was too tired."

Elisa took it in without comment.

Alex said. "I've never given you the grand tour. Would you like to see the grounds before it gets too dark?"

A slight frown cropped up on Elise's face. "Well, I'd love to see Bear Rocks, but I'm going to need more time to explore than the daylight we have left. Can we walk up to the top of the lighthouse instead?"

Alex nodded. "We might have to share the view with someone else. A lot of townsfolk have been coming to see the murder scene. Do you mind?"

Elise placed her hand delicately on Alex's arm. "Oh, Alex. I'm sorry. That's probably the last place in the world you want to be so soon after your friend's death. We can go some other time."

"The lighthouse means a lot to me. I hate that someone used it as a place to kill Reg, but there have been deaths there before. The old stone walls just absorb it all, the good along with the bad."

As they walked outside and over to the steps, Elise said, "Tell me who else died here. Goodness, I sound ghoulish, don't I?"

Alex shook his head. "It's part of the lighthouse history. Fifty years ago, a couple of kids were stopped from eloping by their parents. Before anyone knew what was happening, they broke into the tower and climbed the steps together. It was the last thing they did in this lifetime. Dad found their bodies at the base the next morning. Some of the people in town wanted the inn closed because of the deaths, as if it was somehow the lighthouse's fault."

Elise said, "That's so unfair. If someone wants to kill

himself, there are surely more ways to do it than leaping from the top pf a lighthouse."

They were just starting to climb the first level of the stairs when Barb Matthews came racing down the final steps toward them. Instead of a greeting, she started attacking Alex.

"Where were you today? I needed fresh linen and had to scrounge it myself. What kind of inn are you running, anyway? I hear someone else almost died today, a fact you neglected to share with me. Who's next? Me? 'Gas leak' my foot. You can't pull anything over on me, Mr. Winston. I'm too sharp for that."

Alex bit back his first response. He knew perfectly well Elise had been at the inn all day. It was obvious Barb Matthews just wanted something to complain about. "I'm sorry about the linen, but we've got a lot going on right now. If you aren't happy with your accommodations at Hatteras West, I'd be glad to make alternate arrangements someplace in town for you." Alex offered his slickest smile to the woman.

She tapped him squarely in the chest with the dragonhead cane. It surprised Alex that she carried the walking stick up the steps of the lighthouse when there was a handrail on either side of staircase, but Mrs. Matthews was obviously a law unto herself.

She scowled and said, "You're not getting rid of me that easily, Mr. Winston. I'm planning to stay here till they drag my body out. You understand?"

Alex barely refrained from snapping a salute. "Yes Ma'am. I've got it."

Mrs. Matthews started to leave through the red doors when Alex called out, "By the way, we'll both be out of the inn tomorrow morning, so you'd better make your linen requests tonight."

She whirled around. "Where do you think you're going, young man? In case you've forgotten, you've got a business to run."

Alex offered his open palms in a plea. "We're going rockhounding. Care to join us?"

The look of pale contempt she shot him as she walked away was far greater than Alex ever imagined he actually deserved. Or maybe Reg's murder had made him a little more sensitive than normal.

Elise smiled lightly after the woman was gone. "Oh, you're bad. You couldn't get her out of here now with a crowbar."

"Look at that. It's like a wave of clouds coming right at us."

Alex had been watching Elise as she drank in the surrounding hills from high atop the lighthouse's upper balcony. He pulled his gaze away from her and saw a massive flank of clouds rolling down the mountain toward them like spilled liquid marshmallow.

Alex said, "It's really something, isn't it? 'The fog rolls in like silent thunder, dressing the trees in liquid smoke.'"

Elise turned towards Alex. "Who wrote that?"

Alex admitted, "That's from one of the poems I wrote in high school. There used to be a lot more of it, but I'm afraid I've forgotten the rest."

Elise's eyes went back to the hills. "It's exactly what a real lighthouse should see. Instead of the ocean, we've got the clouds."

In a few minutes, the ground was covered with the low-lying fog. Only at the observation level could Alex see clearly. It was like flying in an airplane, only better. This particular trip didn't cost a thing, and there was no risk of crashing.

Alex touched the railing with his hands. "I used to come up here to get away from everything. Dad finally gave me a key to keep me from taking his all the time. I'm not sure Mom ever knew where I disappeared to, but I suspect Dad told her. I always figured this was Dad's secret place as a boy, too but we never talked about it. It was one of the few close bonds we had. He loved Hatteras West as much as I do. Before the town built up so much, my favorite reason to come here was because of the stars. Elise, they were breathtaking. Looking up into the night, it was like the sky was on fire. I swear you could almost read by their light. Then slowly, Elkton Falls began to grow. As it did, the town lights stole more and more of the sky from us." Alex gestured to the sky. "It's still magnificent, but it's more like a faded flower, just a reflection of the beauty that I remember."

Alex realized he had talked for an awfully long time. When he glanced at Elise, he saw her eyes were on him instead of the magnificence around them.

Alex shrugged. "I'm sorry. I always get carried away up here. Especially at night."

Elise smiled softly. "I bet your girlfriends loved it here."

Alex grinned. "Do you want to know the truth? You're the first person I've ever brought up here at night."

"Not even Sandra?" Elisa asked.

"She wants me to sell out to Finster's client. Sandra never has understood the pull Hatteras West has on me."

Elise said softly, "How can she not feel it?"

In the next moments of silence, Alex had to fight the urge to kiss her. He wanted to, there was no doubt about that. Elise's presence had made Alex realize that he and Sandra weren't going to be together much longer. Though they'd been a couple off and on for a long time, there wasn't the bond there that he'd already formed with Elise.

It was a shame she was engaged to someone else.

With a false air of casualness, he said, "Would you like to see the Fresnel lens work?"

Elise suddenly turned into a little girl. "Can we? I thought you said the town banned it."

Alex grinned. "In this fog, they won't care. Besides, it's still early."

"Let's do it. Can I light the wick?"

Alex smiled. "You could if we had one. Dad converted the lamp to electricity thirty years ago."

"Show me what to do."

Alex led Elise down to the watch room just below the lantern itself. On one wall there was a lonely two-button switch, much like one found in the average home of the forties. Elise didn't look impressed. "That's it? I expected something more."

"Push the top button in."

Elise did as she was told, and suddenly the tiny room was filled with bright light. Alex led Elise onto the lower observation platform where they could see the beam cutting into the growing night. Its brilliance was overwhelming. They watched it for a few moments as it started to rotate, then Alex went back inside and hit the lower button, cutting off the lens's power.

He rejoined Elise outside and explained, "Dad hooked up a motor to turn the Fresnel lens instead of the weights they used to use. I try to keep the beam pointed away from town. It's beautiful, isn't it?"

"Let me tell you when I get my eyesight back. Wow, I can't believe how bright it is."

Alex took her hand and led her inside to an old wooden bench that hugged one wall. "The beam will blind you if you're standing in the wrong spot up there, but it's a magical sight, especially in the fog."

Suddenly, a shout rang out from below.

"Decent folk are trying to sleep down here. Keep that overgrown night-light off, you durn fool."

The voice unmistakably belonged to Barb Matthews. The moment between them had passed.

Alex and Elise walked down the steps of the lighthouse and headed back for their separate rooms. Back inside the inn, Elise quickly said, "I had a lovely evening, Alex. Good night." And then she was gone.

13

The next morning, Alex had just gotten dressed when he heard a timid knock on his door. It was Elise.

She said, "Good, you're awake. Listen, I just saw Junior drive off, so if we want to follow him, we need to go right now."

Some detective he was. Alex had forgotten all about trailing Junior this morning. "Let me grab my keys and we'll go."

Even though they were in a hurry, Alex managed to find time to hold Elise's door for her.

As they headed down the road, he asked, "Have you eaten anything?"

She opened her large handbag. "No, but I packed a few bananas and an apple I got yesterday at the store, and I filled a thermos with hot coffee. Want to share with me?"

"That sounds good. It would be nice if we could grab a biscuit, too, but I'm not positive Junior's really going rockhounding. Still, it's a good thing you dressed for a dig."

Elise wore a faded pair of jeans and a work shirt that had probably belonged to her father. He hoped it wasn't her fiancé's. Alex desperately wanted to ask her about the mystery man in her life, but he just couldn't find the words. Had he imagined her interest in him up in the lighthouse the night before? He had to admit that Elise could have been under the beacon's spell, too. Now, in the cold light of day, he wondered if she'd regretted their lost opportunity as much as he did.

Alex studied her a second as he drove. She had on a sturdy pair of work boots, and her lustrous hair was pulled back into a ponytail, secured by a wide band of red cloth that matched the shirt she wore.

Elise said, "You warned me what we might be doing. I debated on wearing Dad's old shirt, but I didn't really have anything else appropriate. I usually don't look this ragged."

Alex smiled. "I think you look fine." Glorious, wonderful, stunning, he substituted, but only in his mind.

Alex himself was dressed much the same. He had grown up digging in the hills around the valley, hoping to match his great-grandfather's find. All he'd ever managed to come up with were tiny chips of ruby and emerald, a carload of smoky quartz and even some Hiddenite, a greenish rock found only in the area they would be digging.

Elise shared a banana and then said, "Tell me what to expect. I've never been rockhounding before."

"Well, a lot of it depends on where Junior goes. I've been to Emerald Valley before, and they've got their commercial operation down cold. You can dig up on the mountain, what they call the 'mining area,' or you can sluice a pail full of dirt they provide, for a fee of course."

"It's not very likely there will be anything in one of those, is it?"

Alex grinned. "Don't bet on it. Just about every bucket on the place has been salted with one stone or another, unless you tell them otherwise."

He looked over to find a puzzled expression on Elise's face. She said, "That doesn't make any sense. How can they make any money if they give their stones away?"

Alex laughed. "What they give away are large common stones, usually not worth much of anything. But the tourists feel lucky unearthing a hunk of smoky quartz, so they buy another bucket."

"Why, that's not honest at all." Alex didn't need to see Elise's face. He could hear the outrage in her voice.

"I used to think so myself. But if you know the right questions to ask, they'll tell you the truth. Some of the buckets are 'guaranteed,' those are the ones that are salted, and some of them are 'native.' It works. You have to remember, if there was much hope of finding anything valuable, they'd operate as a real mine instead of a tourist attraction. Some tourists have surprised them though, pulling a real quality stone out of one of their buckets. It's happened more than once."

Elise shook her head. "I still don't like it. It just doesn't seem like a fair hunt."

Alex nodded his agreement. "If it's fair you want, I'll take you down the creek away from the main area. Whatever you find there is pretty likely to be a genuine find."

"Well, at least they don't salt the creek."

Alex laughed. "Don't kid yourself. Every time a busload of tourists come in, they scatter a handful of gem fragments right at the creek entrance. It must be working, because people keep coming back for more. It's harmless enough, if you know the ground rules."

Elise still seemed a little put off by the arrangement. Alex protested, "Hey, if you're going to think badly of them, you probably wouldn't have cared much for my father. I told you he salted our land with quite a few fragments hoping it would help the inn."

"I believe I'll side with your mother on that one."

Alex chuckled softly. "Mom nearly skinned him alive. She made Dad go out and look for every stone he'd planted. I can still see the sheepish look on his face, but to this day, I can't tell if it was from his actions, or just because he got caught. I could never prove anything, but I don't think he ever stopped salting the land; he enjoyed it too much, and there are a lot more stones around the inn than the times Dad admitted to. I don't know, with Dad, it was always hard to tell when he was serious and when he was just having a little fun."

Elise said grudgingly, "Okay, I guess I can understand that. Promise me one thing, though. I want you to take me where no one has salted any stones, okay? If I find something, I want to be sure it's legitimate."

Alex nodded. "If that's where Junior goes, we'll go there, too."

They drove on in companionable silence. Alex finally caught sight of Junior's car on the road up ahead. It was pulled off to the side, and Alex could see Junior leaning against the hood. He thought about passing, but when he saw Junior's slumped shoulders, he pulled his truck in behind him on an impulse.

Elise said, "Alex, he's crying."

"I know. Do you want to come with me, or should I go talk to him alone?"

Elise paused in thought. "Why don't you go? You knew his father, and he might feel uncomfortable with me there, too."

Alex patted Elise's hand and got out of the truck. Only when the truck door squeaked did Junior look up to see Alex walking toward him. He tried to wipe away his tears, but quickly gave up.

Obviously embarrassed, Junior said, "Um, Alex. What are you doing out here?"

"I thought I'd take Elise rock hunting since she's never been before."

Junior glanced at Elise and waved slightly. Alex could see the man's discomfort at having been caught in such an emotional state.

Gamely, Junior said, "I was going to try it myself. I thought it might take my mind off all that has happened. Then it started to sink in that Dad's really gone." A few sniffles escaped. "Alex, my father wasn't the easiest man in the world to get along with, and it didn't help that he was my boss as well as my dad." Junior stifled back a sob, then added, "I don't know how I'm going to manage without him."

Alex said, "Surely he's been grooming you to take over for some time. Reg always talked about retiring up here so he could be closer to the inn."

Junior snorted. "Don't believe a word of it, Alex, he loved his work. Not only that, but I don't think the company will survive without him. Dad was the glue that held everything together. I don't care about that right now. I just want to mourn him as his son."

Alex patted Junior on the shoulder and said, "Listen there's a diner about two miles ahead. Why don't we all get a bite of breakfast?"

Junior wiped his face with a handkerchief. Alex noticed that the man really was fastidious about his appearance. He began to guiltily wonder if Junior could have actually found a clean spot on the loop trail to take a nap. It didn't explain the grass-stained outfit he had given Armstrong, but could Junior simply have made a mistake? Were these tears because of the man's loss, or motivated by remorse for killing his own father? Now Alex somehow doubted that Junior could have done it.

Junior tucked the handkerchief back into his pocket. "Thanks, but I don't want to spoil your plans. Why don't you two go ahead? I'm going back to the inn to pack. It's too tough staying there, Alex. Everywhere I look, I see something Dad loved."

Alex said, "Why don't we head back with you? Suddenly I don't feel so easy leaving the inn at a time like this. We'll put on a pot of tea and see if we can convince Elise to make something special. She's really a great cook."

Junior smiled slightly. "That would be nice. I'll follow you back."

As Junior got into his car, Alex headed to the truck. Elise had a puzzled look on her face.

He said, "We're going back."

Elise managed to hide her disappointment. "Why, what's going on?"

Before starting the truck, Alex leaned over and

looked her straight in the eye. "Elise, do you believe in hunches?"

"Sometimes that's all we have to go by. Why?"

Alex repeated his conversation with Junior after he started the truck and headed back toward the inn. "I don't believe that man had anything to do with his father's death. He's too torn up right now. I believe he's sincere."

Elise said, "You told me he said himself he can't run the business without his father. Could it be the enormity of what he's done has finally hit home?"

Alex shrugged. "I don't know. I've got to admit that thought crossed my mind. I still don't think he killed Reg, though."

They were just pulling on to Point Road when Alex saw the smoke.

Elise caught sight of it at the same time.

She said, "Is someone burning leaves and branches this early in the fall?"

Alex clenched his hands on the steering wheel as he raced up the road. He knew nobody near him did any regular burning this time of year. Besides the land that Alex had, the rest of the acreage surrounding Hatteras West was owned by people who lived out of state. That left the smoke coming from somewhere too close to home.

Alex felt a sickness in the pit of his stomach that made talking impossible. In two minutes, his worst fears were confirmed. As they pulled into sight of the two structures where guests stayed, only one building remained standing. The main keeper's house, the place

Alex had grown up and spent his formative years in, was burned to the ground.

From the look of things, only the dedicated work of the town volunteer fire department had managed to save the other building, now a lone twin left standing beside the lighthouse. Alex felt himself crying as he stopped the truck away from the firefighters. The pile of rubble, still smoldering under the steady stream of water from the fire truck, held just about every tangible memory of Alex's childhood.

And now it was all gone.

14

Alex looked up to see Mor approach the truck. At first, it was hard for Alex to recognize him; the big man was covered with ashes and black soot. Alex stumbled out of the truck and nearly fell when his feet hit the ground.

"What happened?" His throat was raw as his gaze swept across the burned ruins.

Mor said, "We're still not sure, but the chief says it looks like arson."

"Arson?" That thought had never crossed Alex's mind. Unlike the original it had been based on, the structure had been nearly solid wood, from the walls to the floors to the ceilings to the exterior. He had assumed that faulty wiring or something of that nature had destroyed the building. "My God, who would want to burn down my inn?"

Mor coughed lightly. "Were there any guests in the main house? I hate to ask, but we need to know."

Alex blew out a sigh of relief. "No, we were slow, so

I decided to keep everyone in the annex. I thought it would be easier to keep track of everybody that way."

Mor looked visibly relieved. "Excuse me a minute, I'll go tell the chief. He'll be glad to hear it."

Elise had quietly joined Alex. The two of them stood in silence, staring at the still-smoking ground where the main keeper's house had once stood. Alex yearned to sift through the debris, searching for any lost relic of his past, but Elise gently restrained him, keeping her hand on his shoulder.

She said, "When everyone's gone and the ashes have cooled, I'll help you look for anything we can salvage."

Alex said, "Do you think there's a chance the fire had anything to do with Reg's murder and what happened to Emma?"

"Don't say anything to Armstrong about it. He still doesn't believe Emma's fall was really a push."

Alex twisted around and looked deeply into her eyes. "You believe me, don't you, Elise?"

She said softly, "Something strange is going on around here, but if we're going to convince anyone else, we're going to have to get proof first."

A shiny black Porsche pulled up to the inn, probably a tourist trying to see what had caused the black towers of smoke. Alex didn't pay it any attention, but Elise suddenly dropped her hand from Alex's shoulder.

"What's wrong," he asked her as a tall, handsome man with longish blonde hair got out.

Instead of answering, Elise hurried to him. "Peter. What are you doing here?"

Alex was close enough to hear them as the man said, "I was worried about you. Your cousin told me you were out here! When I saw the smoke, I was afraid I'd lost you forever." He hugged her tightly, and Alex felt a tug of jealousy. Peter had to be the mysterious fiancé.

Elise broke from the embrace, then led her fiancé to Alex. "Alex Winston, this is Peter Asheford. Peter, this is my new boss, Alex."

"So it's true, you're actually working as a maid," Peter said to Elise after shaking Alex's hand briefly. "Elise, we need to talk about this. Can we go somewhere?"

"Excuse me," Alex said. "I've got to see about what's left of my inn."

All hopes of winning Elise's heart were gone for Alex. He knew he couldn't compete with Peter Asheford in looks or money. The way the man gazed at her, it was obvious he was in love with her.

Elise said, "Peter, Alex needs me here."

Alex absently waved a hand in the air. "There's nothing you can do, Elise. Go with him."

Elise looked startled by his answer, but Peter jumped on the response. As he steered Elise toward the Porsche, he said, "There's a quaint little diner in town. Let's go have a cup of coffee. I've missed you so much, Elise."

As the sports car drove away, Sam Finster's Cherokee passed it on the driveway of Hatteras West.

Finster's sympathy was as natural as machine-made snow, and just about as warming, too. Surveying the damage, he shook his head from side to side.

"It's a darn shame losing such a fine old building. Have you kept your insurance paid up?"

Alex ignored the question. "How'd you hear about the fire, Finster?"

The man cracked a smile. "I've got my sources. To get ahead, a fella's got to stay on top of things in this old world." Alex figured the vulture had most likely been eavesdropping on his police scanner. It was reported to be one of Finster's best sources for leads. The second a homeowner died, Finster was at the funeral home making arrangements with the grieving widow to sell the home.

Finster repeated, "Alex, this is important. Is your insurance healthy?"

The man was relentless. Alex said, "If you're worried about your clients losing interest in the property, don't. It's inevitable. I couldn't afford replacement value on my policy, so I won't be attempting to rebuild it. I don't know how much I'll be getting, but I know it won't be enough to cover all of this damage."

Without the extra money those rooms brought in during peak season, he was finished as an innkeeper. The wisest thing to do was to see if the buyer would still be interested in acquiring the property, at a reduced rate of course, then take the insurance money and leave Elkton Falls forever.

No one had ever accused Alex of doing the wisest thing.

Finster must have misinterpreted Alex's expression. He leaned forward in a conspirator's gesture. "Tell you what I'll do. Let's go down to my office as soon as everybody leaves. You can sign the offer sheet, I'll date it yesterday, and nobody will have to be the wiser. That way this setback won't touch you. You can pass the loss off to the new owner. It's a sweet deal, Alex. You'd better jump on it."

Alex didn't try to keep the disgust from his face. "That would increase your cut of the commission, too, wouldn't it?"

Finster stroked his chin. "Hey, you win, I win. Who cares about the buyer? What do you say, have we got a deal?"

Alex had suddenly reached his limit. All of his anger shot out at Finster.

Alex jammed his index finger hard into the real estate man's chest. "Get the hell off my property this instant. If I so much as see your Cherokee anywhere near Point Road, I'll run you into the bushes. Now go."

Finster started toward his car, then turned back. His face livid, he shouted, "You'll be sorry for threatening me, I'm a big man around these parts."

Alex yelled, "Finster, get out before I kick your fat ugly butt all the way back to the town limits."

Finster hurried to his Cherokee and drove off in a spray of gravel. Alex turned to find several of the firefighters cheering heartily. A chorus of "Yeah, Alex" and "Way to tell that old windbag" accompanied him as he joined their ranks. Somehow the confrontation had left Alex feeling dirty. He hated losing his temper.

The fire chief cut Alex out of the crowd and pulled him toward the back of the remains of the building. The firefighters took it as a cue to go back to work patrolling the area immediately surrounding the burned building.

Chief Weston was a small, wiry man who looked like an elf in a Christmas parade. Alex had personally seen the man lift timbers that would have stymied Mor Pendleton.

The chief looked coolly into Alex's eyes. "You just made yourself one mouthy enemy there."

Alex grunted. "He's had it coming for a long time. Finster just picked the wrong man to go after today."

Chief Weston nodded once. "I couldn't agree with

you more. Still and all, you'd better watch your step around that fellow."

"I don't think I'll have any more trouble from him, Chief, but thanks for the advice." Alex kicked at some of the rubble at his feet. "Mor tells me you think this is arson."

The little man nodded in agreement. "They didn't try to hide it too hard, either. We found a gas can overturned by the back part of the house."

"So whoever set the blaze couldn't be seen from the lighthouse."

The chief said, "That's about right. I hear you're having your share of troubles over here."

Alex offered a weak smile. "That's putting it mildly. Did one of my guests call the alarm in? I want to thank them myself."

A puzzled expression crossed the fire chief's face. "That's kind of curious. Mor Pendleton telephoned to say he was out here and for everyone to come quick. From what I hear around town, he'd been spending quite a bit of his free time at the inn." The fire chief scratched his chin. "You should be glad he saw the flare-up in time. Otherwise you could have lost everything but the lighthouse."

Weston's wife ran the town's only pet-grooming salon, so it didn't surprise Alex that the man had the latest word on everyone's behavior, in or out of the Elkton Falls city limits. It usually tickled him that the chief was a far worse gossip than his own wife was, but this time it left him cold. Was Mor after Elise, or did he have another, hidden reason for being out at Hatteras West on the morning of a working day? Could Mor have set the fire himself? Surely the man was clever enough to make the job look amateurish, thereby diverting suspicion away from himself. Or maybe he got angry when he found Alex and Elise were gone, so he decided to get a little instant revenge. Blast it all, that didn't sound like the man Alex had grown up with, but infatuation did strange things to people sometimes.

Weston interrupted his thoughts. "You'd better call Smiley O'Reilly and get him out here." Smiley was the town's oldest insurance agent, and most of the folks had policies with him. Alex had kept paying the premiums after his father's death, but he had no idea what the actual policy was worth.

Alex agreed and headed toward the remaining part of the inn. He was almost to the front porch when Chief Weston called out his name. As Alex turned, he saw Smiley's old Chevy pickup drive up. It was possibly the only running truck in the county in even worse condition than Alex's own transportation. The vehicles had been a running joke between the two men for a long time.

Smiley popped out of the truck, awfully spry for a man just over eighty years old, though he only admitted to being seventy-eight.

Smiley glanced at the smoldering remnants, shook his head sadly and said, "Heard about the blaze. Figured I might save you a call." The man invariably dropped the first word or two of every sentence he spoke, and Alex quickly found himself slipping easily into the pattern whenever the two of them talked.

"Good of you to come, Smiley."

The old man grinned through a set of perfect dentures. "Saw Finster. Mad as a wet hornet."

Alex laughed, consciously fighting the urge to continue Smiley's speech pattern. "He's been after me to sell the place for a while now. I must admit, I probably should have taken him up on it."

Smiley looked grim for the first time Alex could remember.

Alex asked, "Is there something wrong?"

"About your policy. Should have been more. Doesn't amount to much."

Alex felt his blood run cold. He had suspected the premiums were ridiculously low, but truthfully, he had barely managed to pay them as it was.

"Go ahead and give me the bad news. I'm in shock now anyway."

Smiley looked down at the dirt. "Twenty thousand worth of coverage."

"For the entire building? You've got to be kidding. The wood alone was worth more than that as salvage."

Smiley looked even more miserable. "Don't understand. Twenty thousand maximum. Buildings, furnishings, whole blamed property, lighthouse and all."

Alex couldn't believe what he was hearing. "What? How could that be possible?"

Smiley started squirming. "My fault. Should have got you to carry more. Knew you probably couldn't afford it. Didn't ask."

Alex's head began to throb. Twenty thousand dollars. Just a portion of the land he owned, even undeveloped, was worth that. Finster's offer was starting to look awfully good, and for a moment Alex regretted his abrupt behavior. No. No matter how bad things got, he wasn't about to do business with a rat like Sam Finster.

Alex said, "It's not your fault, Smiley. You were

right, I couldn't have afforded any more insurance than I carried."

Smiley had a small expression of relief on his face. "Get the money to you soon. Shouldn't have to wait."

"Don't worry about it, old friend."

Alex walked Smiley back to his truck and leaned in through the driver's side window. "Do you think this jalopy will make it back into town, or should I follow you in case you don't make it?"

Smiley shook his head slightly, the grin slowly returning to his face. "Wouldn't suggest it. Just have to run you back out here when yours died. See you."

Alex watched as Smiley drove off. Several of the firefighters were starting to leave, and Alex took a few moments to thank them for their help. He noticed Mor hanging around.

Alex said, "I heard you were the one to call in the fire. Thanks. What were you doing out here in the middle of the morning, anyway?"

Mor managed to look the slightest bit sheepish, while being defensive at the same time. "I came over to ask Elise out again. I wasted a trip, didn't I? That must have been her fiancé in the Porsche. Man, I know I can't compete with that." The handyman glanced at his watch and said, "I'd better get back to the shop before Les has to actually do a little work himself."

As Mor joined some of the other firefighters in a truck that was pulling out, Alex glanced back at the remaining building. He saw a flurry of curtains on the top floor of what was left of his inn. Those rooms were open and unoccupied, and Alex wondered who could be watching him.

He was just heading for the door to investigate when

Chief Weston approached him. Alex noticed that he was the last firefighter to leave the site. "Well, I believe we got it all."

Alex shook the little man's hand. "Thanks for everything, Chief."

Before leaving, Weston offered one last piece of advice. "I'd watch my step if I were you. Someone's got it in for Hatteras West. I just hope they don't finish the job they started today."

15

Alex was surprised to realize that he was hungry, despite the loss he'd just suffered. He decided to slap a sandwich together, grab a Coke from the fridge and go eat on Bear Rocks. He needed some time alone away from the burned wreckage to pull himself together.

He'd forgotten all about his plans for lunch with Sandra until he saw her car coming up the road.

When she got out, she said, "What happened to our lunch date?"

"I forgot all about it." Was it possible she didn't even notice that one of his buildings was gone?

"I heard about the fire. I'm sorry, Alex. Why don't we go get something to eat and we can talk about what you should do next."

"There's nothing to discuss. I just need some time alone, Sandra."

She raised one eyebrow. "Time alone, or alone with your new maid?"

"She's off with her fiancé, Sandra."

The smug look on her face was too much for Alex. He added, "Not that it matters. I don't know how to say this, but I don't think we should see each other any more. You and I want different things out of life."

Sandra stared intently at him. "You don't mean that, Alex, you're just distraught over the fire." She smiled lightly, then said, "Everything will look better tomorrow," as she started to get back into her car.

"I'm not going to change my mind, Sandra. I'm sorry. It's over."

Sandra realized suddenly that he was quite serious. She snapped, "Do you think if you're suddenly free your little maid will drop her fiancé for you, Alex? It's not going to happen."

"Good-bye, Sandra," Alex said.

She started to say something, changed her mind then pulled furiously out of the parking lot.

Finally, Alex was alone.

He was surprised to find that the only thing he felt was relief. Breaking up with Sandra had been a long time coming, and he tried to convince himself that it had nothing to do with Elise.

He was only partially successful.

Eating alone was not to be, though. Joel Grandy spotted Alex leaving the inn and asked if he could join him. Reluctantly, Alex agreed. The two men walked out to the granite rocks in silence. Alex could still smell smoke in the air.

Grandy said, "That was really some fire today. With all that wood in the walls and ceilings, it was bound to happen sooner or later."

Grandy's words brought Alex out of his own thoughts, and he didn't care for the implications of the man's comments. "The fire chief said it was arson. Nobody can prevent that, Mr. Grandy."

Grandy tried to calm Alex with his words. "Say, get your feathers back down, boy, I didn't mean anything by it. The reason I've tagged along out here is that I've been thinking about something I've been wanting to discuss with you, but it's been tough getting you off by yourself."

Alex, not caring to pursue the conversation, climbed up and perched in the lap of one of the boulders. Someone in his family had called it Mamma Bear Rock a long time ago, and sitting in the cradle of the stone, he could see why. The warm sun felt good on his face.

Alex took out his sandwich. "Sorry I can't offer you much more than half of this."

Grandy waved it away. "I had a big breakfast at Buck's in town. You go ahead and eat. We can talk after you're done."

Grandy watched Alex finish his sandwich before speaking again. "I've grown kind of fond of this place, the lighthouse and all, and I was wondering if you'd consider selling it to me."

Alex looked at Joel Grandy with new interest. "You wouldn't happen to be represented by a real estate agent in town named Finster, would you?"

Grandy snorted. "I don't have an agent, Alex. I'm asking you man to man. What would you take for the place?"

Alex shook his head. "It's not for sale." He made sure the tone in his voice was as uninviting as he could make it.

Joel Grandy leaned back against an upright rock and said, "I've been wheeling and dealing a long time, Alex, and one thing I've learned is that everything on this globe is for sale if the price and the conditions are right. What would you say to two hundred grand?"

Alex didn't have any idea if Joel Grandy was just talking big, or if he actually had the funds to back up his offer. It didn't matter to Alex either way. "I'd say someone else offered me two hundred and fifty thousand dollars this morning."

Instead of putting Grandy off, Alex's words elicited a laugh from the man that sounded like a donkey with a doughnut stuck in his throat. "Okay, then. How about an even three hundred thousand? I admit I was lowballing you, Alex. I hope you don't mind my saying it, but you're craftier than you look."

Alex studied the man in silence, not trusting himself to speak.

Grandy spoke for him. "Oh, I get it. You don't think I could raise that kind of money, do you? Let me show you something about not judging a book by its cover." Grandy pulled a statement out of his pocket from a stockbrokerage house that showed his share value as of the first of the month.

"I had this sent down just in case you needed convincing."

Alex saw that Grandy's offer would barely put a dent in even one of the man's holdings.

"Why would you want an old lighthouse and some granite rocks?"

Grandy grinned at him. "I could tell you it's the lighthouse itself that draws me, but that's only part of it. I like these rocks, to be honest with you. They touch something in me I thought was long dead. I came out here in the fog last night, and I swear to you they seemed to come alive and dance in the mist. It took my breath away. There are other reasons that I'll tell you straight out are none of your business, but I will say that my grandkids would love that tower of yours over there. Can you imagine a better fort than that?"

Alex smiled. "Yes, I rescued my fair share of maidens there in my mind. Seriously, though, why buy the place? You could rent the inn for a month at a time and have Hatteras West all to yourself."

Grandy rubbed the rock he was sitting on affectionately for a moment before answering. "Renting and owning are two different things. I want these rocks."

Alex knew the feeling well. "Thanks for your interest, but none of my land is for sale."

The older man stood up abruptly from his seat. "It's not the money, is it?"

"Not entirely."

Grandy thought about that for a moment. "Give it some thought anyway, and we'll talk again. One thing, though." He stuck one bony finger in the air toward Alex, and he could see a flicker of heat in Grandy's eyes. "Don't sell to anybody else without talking to me first. I wouldn't want you to get hurt on the deal."

"Is that a threat, Mr. Grandy?"

In an instant, the look of fire was hidden again in the old man's eyes. Alex didn't buy the "doddering old grandfather" routine for a minute.

Grandy eased his voice as he said, "Why would an old man like me threaten a young pup like you? I just meant that you shouldn't take another offer without giving me a chance to put in my bid, that's all. I might surprise you."

As Alex watched Joel Grandy walk back down the path toward the inn, he silently admitted to himself that the old man had already surprised him. Alex kicked himself for not asking Grandy where he'd been when the fire had started this morning. As an amateur detective, he was turning out to be a failure.

No matter. Alex leaned back fully into Mamma Bear's lap and let the heat from the sunshine-warmed granite seep into his bones.

He nearly fell asleep from the soothing warmth, but a sudden shift in the wind brought him fully back to his senses.

As he lay there, Alex decided to review the suspects who could have possibly killed Reg and started the fire, too.

Junior was out as a suspect, not just because Alex couldn't believe the man had killed his own father, but because Alex had followed him all morning. Unless, of course, the younger Wellington knew how to start a delayed fire, which would allow him to torch the inn while establishing a perfect alibi for himself.

Alex knew there had to be a hundred different ways to accomplish a delayed blaze, though he didn't have a clue how one would go about it. Reluctantly, he decided that Junior had to remain a suspect until more evidence came to light.

Alex then considered Joel Grandy. Could he have started the blaze in order to motivate Alex to sell the property? Then why did he kill Reg? He thought about the other people who had been around. Barb Matthews might have burned down the building out of sheer cussedness, Finster was that mean too, but neither one of them had an apparent reason to kill Reg.

As much as Alex hated to consider the prospect, Mor could have easily set the fire before reporting it. But then again, why kill Reg? And how did Emma Sturbridge's fall factor into the equation?

Perhaps Armstrong and Hicking were right about Emma's fall. It could have been an accident. He wished she would come out of her coma so she could tell him what had really happened.

By the time Alex was ready to go back to the inn, it was late afternoon. Already the sun had started its decline behind a large stand of white pines that bordered the western edge of the property. As he started to get up, Alex felt something in his neck catch. He tried to work the kink out by moving his head back and forth, but it didn't seem to help at all.

He really shouldn't have stayed away from the inn so long. For the first time since taking over Hatteras West, Alex had put his own concerns ahead of those of his guests. He walked stiffly down the path to the inn, pausing only for a moment to survey the scorched earth where the main keeper's house had stood. The ground was nothing but a black, soggy mess.

When Alex entered the remaining building, he nearly ran into Barb Matthews. Her eyes lit up the second she saw Alex. "Can't you protect your guests? That fire could have easily spread to this building. You know that, don't you?"

Alex smiled thinly. "It's good to see you escaped the fire unharmed, Mrs. Matthews."

"Unharmed? I've been coughing up soot and smoke ever since those firemen came." The woman tapped her dragonhead cane on Alex's chest. "No help from you, that's for sure. If it weren't for that handsome young man warning us about the fire, we might have all perished."

It looked like there was a new Mor Pendleton fan.

Alex said gently, "I'm just glad everyone's safe."

When the woman saw that Alex wasn't going to rise to her bait, she stormed out the front door.

Junior came out of the hallway and said, "Good, she's gone." He rubbed his chest gently. "She tapped me so hard I think she left a bruise."

Alex smiled slightly. "She's a real ray of sunshine, isn't she?"

Junior said, "Do you have any plans for dinner? We could grab a quick bite and play a little chess, if you're interested. It might take our minds off our troubles."

Alex was suddenly glad for the older man's company. He made a couple of sandwiches in his kitchenette while Junior set up the chessboard.

Alex carried the platter of sandwiches out to the lobby.

Junior surveyed the offering with a smile. "Now all we need is something to drink."

Alex could name a few other things he needed more, but he suddenly remembered life had been no picnic for his dinner companion, either. The man had just lost his father and was now the sheriff's prime suspect in the murder investigation.

Alex went back to the refrigerator and pulled out two Cokes. As he handed one to Junior, he asked, "Sorry I'm out of beer. How are you holding up?"

A frown crossed the man's face. Junior said, "For some reason, the police refuse to release Dad's body.

He always wanted to be cremated, so as soon as they let him go, we'll have a quiet memorial service. Can I ask you a favor, Alex?"

"Name it."

In a steady voice, Junior said, "This was Dad's favorite place on earth. He loved Hatteras West more than he loved his own home. Could we spread his ashes from the observation deck, or do you think that would be too gruesome, considering the fact that he died up there?"

Alex patted Junior's shoulder. "I think Reg would have loved it."

As they ate their meal, Alex told Junior one of his favorite stories about Reg. "I don't know if you're aware of it, but your dad was a real influence on my life. I remember a time when I was twelve years old and in a really rebellious phase of my life against every adult in the world. Every adult except your dad. We took sleeping bags up to the top of the tower one night and decided to stay awake and watch the dawn. Man, the stories he could tell, about his early life growing up, his time in the Marines, everything. He told me how proud he was the first time he saw you after you were born. Your father was a fine man."

Junior shook his head sadly. "You know, you probably knew my father better than anyone else alive. I know he showed you more of himself than he ever did to me."

Alex said, "It's tough between fathers and sons. There are so many expectations. I don't know why he picked me to be his friend, but part of the reason I'm the man I am today is because of him."

Junior nodded as he finished off the rest of his sandwich. "I'd like to stay around long enough to hear those stories Dad told you. Would you mind?"

"Of course not, but I thought you'd already made up your mind about leaving."

Junior said, "Not until I know for sure what happened. Dad would have wanted it that way." He looked intent as he added, "Besides, I really would like to see my father through your eyes."

"I'll do my best." Alex picked up the white queen from the board. "Pick a hand."

Junior was just about to choose when the front door swung open to reveal Sheriff Armstrong, along with SBI agent Sergeant Hicking.

And from the looks on their faces, they weren't there to make a social call.

16

"What can I do for you gentlemen?" Alex asked.

Hicking walked into the room like he was repossessing it. "It's not you we've come to see. Mr. Wellington? We need you to come downtown for some questioning."

Junior looked up in shock. "What is wrong with you people? I swear on all that's holy, I didn't kill my father!"

Hicking said, "I'm not about to get into it here. Now, are you coming peacefully, or are we going to have to do this the hard way?"

Alex stood up. "Surely you don't suspect the man's own son. He told me himself he had nothing to gain from Reg's death except a pound of headaches that come with the business."

Hicking looked surprised. "Don't you consider a million dollars worth of life insurance a good enough motive?"

Junior stammered, "I never knew anything about any insurance. What are you talking about?"

Hicking said, "We'll discuss it downtown, Mr. Wellington."

"Wait a minute," Alex said. "Motive isn't enough. There's no way you can prove he was at the scene of the crime."

Hicking looked smug, while Armstrong had a scowl on his face. The state policeman was evidently acting with the sheriff's forced cooperation.

Hicking said, "There you're wrong. We found a bloodstain on the clothes the sheriff collected earlier. The lab confirms there's a strong possibility it was his father's blood."

Junior said, "This is ridiculous. Dad probably cut himself shaving and brushed up against me. We shared a bathroom here, after all."

Alex said, "It does seem awfully circumstantial, Sergeant."

Hicking ignored Alex completely. "We just want to ask you a few questions, Mr. Wellington, you're not being formally arrested, yet. Now we can do it nice and easy, or we can get rough. But you *are* going with us, make no mistake about that."

Junior got out of his chair and joined the two officers near the door.

Alex called out, "Is there anyone you'd like me to contact?"

As Junior walked out between Armstrong and Hicking, he said, "Don't worry, Alex, I'll call my lawyer from the jail. I didn't kill my father! It's important that you believe me."

Hicking snapped. "It doesn't matter what he thinks. You'd better start concentrating on impressing us."

Alex walked out with the three men. As the SBI

agent moved ahead with Junior, Alex whispered to Armstrong, "Isn't there anything you can do about this?"

"I'm sorry, Alex. My hands are tied. I'll watch out for him, though. Hicking's not a bad guy, he's just eager to make a splash. If Junior didn't kill his father, I won't let him be railroaded for it."

Alex leaned over to speak to Junior as Armstrong helped him into the backseat of the squad car. "For what it's worth, I believe you, Junior."

A look of relief washed over the man's face. Junior's arrest snapped Alex out of his lethargy. He was more determined than ever to find the identity of the real killer. It was most likely the same individual who had started the fire.

Whoever was playing with matches was going to get burned, if Alex had anything to say about it.

Alex was still staring at the unlit logs in the fireplace when Elise walked through the front door. A quick glance at his watch showed Alex it was only 9:30.

Elise didn't see him sitting in the darkness. Once she was inside, she closed the door firmly and leaned her back against it.

Alex said from his corner of the darkness, "Hello."

Elise flipped on the light switch. "Waiting up for me, Alex?"

He shielded his eyes from the intensity of the sudden light. "To be honest with you, I forgot you went out."

"That's not very flattering," she said.

"Where's Peter?" Alex asked softly.

"I don't want to talk about him, Alex."

He said, "That's fine by me." The strain between them was obvious, but Alex didn't know how to relieve it.

Elise rubbed her arms. "It's chilly in here, don't you think? Could we have a fire?" The second she said it, Alex could tell she regretted her word choice. "I'm sorry, I'm sure that's the last thing you want."

"I've got to get over it sooner or later," he said as he lit the fire. As the flames took hold, Alex said, "Hicking and Armstrong came by a few minutes ago and took Junior in for questioning."

Elise shook her head. "That's ridiculous. That man didn't kill his father. I just don't believe it."

Alex said, "That makes two of us. Now all we have to do is figure out who did."

"Then we'll know who burned down the main keeper's quarters. We know the arson was an obvious act of aggression." Elise paused a moment, then added, "Alex, you know it *is* possible that Emma's tumble on the rocks might have just been an accident."

"Maybe, but I'll feel a lot better when she wakes up and we can find out for sure."

Alex brought Elise up to date on everything he'd learned from Chief Weston and Smiley O'Reilly. The air was definitely clearing between them. Elise looked as devastated as Alex felt. When he told her about Grandy's offer, she looked thoughtful.

She said, "It's a little too convenient, him wanting to buy the place right after the fire. Is there any chance he set the blaze himself?"

"I'd be lying if I said the thought never crossed my mind. To be honest with you, I'm more confused than ever. First thing in the morning I'm going to track Finster down and make him tell me who his mystery client is. For some reason, I think that might be the key to this whole mess."

"Alex, have you decided what you're going to do about the long-term plans for the inn? You'll never stay afloat now with those rooms gone."

He smiled. "If you have any life savings tucked away, now would be a really great time to invest in the inn. I'll make you a great deal."

Elise got up from the couch and started pacing around the room. "I don't have any cash, but my grandmother left me some jewelry that might be worth something."

Alex said, "I was just kidding. I can't take your money. If it comes to that, I suppose I could sell Bear Rocks to Grandy. I think that's the only part of the property he's really interested in. I could always ask him if I had to." Alex hated the words the second they were out of his mouth. Bear Rocks meant nearly as much to him as the lighthouse itself. Elise must have seen the hopeless look on his face.

"Don't worry, it's not going to come to that. We'll think of something."

Suddenly the front door banged open.

From the look of Sheriff Armstrong's hat and uniform, it had started to rain outside. Armstrong looked somber as he said, "Any chance I could get a cup of coffee?"

Elise said, "I'll go make a fresh pot."

Armstrong nodded. "Thank you kindly, Ma'am. I'd appreciate that."

As she went to the urn in one corner of the room,

Armstrong lowered his voice. "I didn't want to tell you this in front of Elise. Another body just turned up."

Elise must have been listening anyway. She walked back to the two men without the promised coffee.

She said, "Sheriff, did you say something about finding another body?"

"Go ahead, Sheriff, she's going to find out soon enough. Who was it?"

Armstrong said, "Now that's why I came out here. It was Sam Finster, the real estate man."

Alex moved to the couch and sat down.

Armstrong took off his hat and twirled it in his hands. "Here's the funny part. Somebody called in an anonymous tip and told us where to look for the Cherokee. We get lots of crank calls, but we check them all out anyway. Would you like to guess where we found him?"

Alex shook his head. "I'm more curious about how he died. Care to share that information with me?"

Staring intently into Alex's face, the sheriff said, "Tell you what, I'll give you both facts and see what you think. We found Finster in his Cherokee about a mile away from here in the peach grove. It looks like whoever got your friend Reg took Finster out the same way."

The grove. Peaches had been one of his grandmother's favorite projects around the property, so the family history went. Apples would have been a better crop for the area, but it had been said that Alex's grandfather had never learned to say "no" to his wife.

The family's landholdings were once quite a bit more extensive than the present property. Alex knew the current owner of that particular parcel of land, a man named Eggars who lived in Florida. Alex had even managed to get permission to pick peaches during the season whenever there was a crop, since Eggars hardly ever came up to North Carolina. He used the land as some sort of tax write-off.

Alex asked, "Any idea about the time of death?"

Armstrong held up his hand. "You're greedy for information, aren't you?"

Alex wasn't in the mood for stonewalling. "I'm also a voter, or have you forgotten about the election?"

"Come on, Alex, take it easy. It's been a rough couple of days around town."

Elise spoke up. "Sheriff, you've got to realize that we have a vested interest in finding out."

"Yes Ma'am, I suppose you do at that. We've got the time of death narrowed down to between 3 and 5 P.M. today. Doc Drake says there's no doubt in his mind that the killer used the same murder weapon as before."

Alex stood up abruptly. "Surely you don't think Junior killed Reg, pushed Emma, set fire to my inn and managed to knock off Finster all in a few days."

Armstrong didn't back down, matching Alex inch-for-inch. "You're living in some kind of fantasy world, son. Get it through your head. Emma Sturbridge fell or slipped, one or the other. Some kid probably torched your inn. We haven't found him yet, but we will, don't you worry about that. As far as Junior Wellington is concerned, pulling him in for questioning was Hicking's idea, not mine. Sam Finster, that's what brings me to the purpose of my visit."

Alex said, "Go on, I'm listening."

The sheriff idly fingered his badge. "There's a rumor

going around town that you threw Finster off your land this very afternoon. I hear it got ugly."

Elise snapped, "You don't believe Alex killed him, do you? I've only been in town a few weeks, and I've already heard of several people who would be more likely to skewer the realtor than Alex would."

Armstrong shrugged. "I don't suppose you have an alibi for this afternoon, do you, Alex?"

Alex looked at the floor. "Actually, I spent the better part of it alone out on Bear Rocks. No one saw me during the hours you're talking about, at least not to my knowledge."

The sheriff nodded. "Those granite stones can be mighty comfy, can't they? You sat around there all afternoon, that's what you're telling me?"

That was all Alex was going to stand for. "Unless you're ready to make an arrest, I suggest you leave the property."

Armstrong headed for the door, but turned back before going through. "Throwing people out is getting to be a habit with you, isn't it, Alex. When I've got more questions, I'll be back. Let me tell you one more thing before I go. I know you don't think much of my detecting abilities, but one fact you can take on faith. If you killed Finster, I'm going to catch you, and I promise you here and now that I'll make sure they nail your hide to the wall."

Elise stepped up. "Spare us the dramatics, Sheriff, and go find the real killer."

The sheriff walked out, and Elise moved back to Alex. After he was gone, Elise said, "What a ridiculous idea. How could anyone seriously believe you killed that man?"

Alex shook his head. "I don't know what's happening around here. It used to be such a quiet, peaceful little town."

"I seem to have brought a lot of trouble with me. Maybe I should have gone back to West Virginia instead of coming here."

Alex touched her arm lightly. "Elise, you're the only good thing to come out of this whole mess. I don't know what I would have done if you hadn't showed up when you did."

"You'd still be drying Marisa's tears, probably. Life would go on." She stifled a yawn. "I'm beat. I'll see you in the morning, Alex. Don't worry, we'll figure this out."

Alex stayed on in the lobby, searching for answers in the dying embers of the fire, He finally got up to make his last circuit of the property, something he did every night before going to sleep. Out on the porch, Alex could smell remnants of the fire in the cool evening air. He thought about going out to check the lighthouse doors to make sure they were locked, but he wearily decided that if another body was anywhere on the property, he didn't want to find it.

Not tonight, anyway.

17

Alex found Elise polishing the front desk when he came out the next morning. "I've got to check on Junior and see how he's holding up," he said. "Do you mind taking care of things here until I get back?"

She shook her head. "Even if we never get another guest, there's enough work around here to last me a month."

"Elise, maybe you should come into town with me. I don't feel right leaving you out here alone while there's a killer on the loose."

"Alex, I'm not going to run and hide just because there's a possibility of danger. Nobody's going to bother me here. Besides, I'll be around people all day."

"I could at least get someone to stay out here with you while I'm gone."

"I've been taking care of myself for a long time, Alex." Her brave front slipped for a moment. "Just come back before it gets dark."

He nodded solemnly. "I promise."

After saying a final good-bye, Alex headed into town to see if the sheriff was still questioning Junior.

As he neared the entrance to one of the property's walking paths, Barb Matthews tried to wave him down, but he pretended he hadn't seen her. There was no way Alex had the stomach to deal with the sour old woman today. He caught a glimpse of her in his rearview mirror, shaking her cane at him as he sped away.

Alex's thoughts went back to Junior. He hoped the line of questions hadn't gotten too intense for Reg's son.

At the courthouse, Alex walked down the steps to the basement, where the police station and jail were both located. The heavy smell of disinfectant reminded Alex of the hospital, and he made a mental note to go check on Emma Sturbridge as soon as he finished with Armstrong.

Behind the glass doors of the sheriff's office, Alex could see the man asleep in a swivel chair, his feet propped up on his desk.

Alex coughed gently, and Armstrong's eyes popped open. The sheriff said, "Been a long night. I didn't mean to fall asleep in the chair. Yow. I think I strained my neck."

Alex remembered the sheriff's attitude with him the night before. He snapped, "Where's Hicking? Is he in taking his turn with the prisoner?"

Armstrong stood up from the chair and stretched. "Naw, he left around midnight. There was a drive-by shooting in Viewpoint." As he dusted himself off, the sheriff said, "Listen Alex, I'm sorry about last night. That trooper's got me so jumpy I'm seeing shadows. You know I don't think you killed Sam Finster. It's just that we've gone a long time with nothing too serious happening around here, and now all at once folks are dropping like flies."

Alex waved it off. "I'll accept your apology if you accept mine. Losing the main keeper's quarters shook me up more than I realized. Is Junior still in the lockup?"

"Take it easy, Alex, we're not going to hold him. There's not enough evidence against him, and he swears up and down he didn't do it. I for one am beginning to believe him."

Alex felt better as soon as he heard the news. "Can I take him back to the inn with me then?"

Armstrong frowned. "I'd really rather you didn't."

"Sheriff, if you're not going to charge him, you've got to let him go. What possible reason do you have to keep holding him here?"

Junior answered that question himself, walking out of the back area in a robe two sizes too big for him and a towel around his neck. It was obvious he'd just gotten out of the shower.

Junior grinned the moment he saw Alex. "I'm going to hang around and give Calvin here a few tips on running his reelection a little more efficiently. I used to be one devil of a campaigner, and I understand our friend has a tight race on his hands. It'll feel good getting my hands into it again."

Armstrong perked up. "Alex, did you know Junior helped run the state campaign for John Anderson's presidential run in 1980? He's a real pro."

Alex decided not to point out that Anderson had run a distant third in that particular race. "That sounds great. You sure you don't mind, Junior? I'd be glad to give you a ride back to the inn. You're not under any obligation to stay here, you know."

Junior managed a weak smile. "I want to do this, Alex. To be honest with you, I see Dad everywhere I look around Hatteras West. This gives me something to do to keep my mind occupied, and I'm close enough if something breaks."

None of it made any sense to Alex, but it seemed the two men had actually worked out some kind of friendship during the night.

Junior coughed politely. "There's just one more thing. Do you think someone could gather up my things and bring them into town for me? I don't feel much like going back to the inn until the memorial service."

"I understand. So you have a place to stay?"

"I'm going to rent a house in town for the time being. I've already made the arrangements."

Alex said, "I thought you'd be getting back to your company."

Junior shook his head. "I'm not leaving until we find out who killed my father. There will be plenty of time to pick up the reins when I get back. In the meantime, the department heads can manage without me." He offered his hand to Alex. "Thanks for believing in me. If there's anything I can ever do for you, just say the word."

For a moment Alex considered asking Junior for a loan so he could rebuild the main keeper's quarters, but owing money to Reg's son would be the same as owing money to the bank, and Alex wasn't about to do that. There had never been any kind of mortgage at Hatteras West, and Alex would continue the tradition, even if it meant he'd be forced to sell the place.

Alex asked Armstrong, "Do you have any other leads on what's been happening at the inn? *Somebody* killed Reg and Finster, and that building didn't burn down by itself."

"Take it easy, Alex. Hicking's requested a full team to look into it. They should be out later on today. I'm in over my head, I admit it. If Hiram Blankenship wants to say I folded under pressure, so be it."

"What are we supposed to do in the meantime, Sheriff? There's a killer on the loose."

"Alex, those SBI guys are the best. They'll catch him; just give them a chance."

Alex left the jail and headed toward his truck in a sudden downpour of rain. After a quick stop at the hospital, he had to get back to the inn. Alex hated leaving Elise alone with a murderer still on the loose, no matter what she said. Maybe he could get someone out there to look after her while he was gone. Who could he call? He couldn't trust the only men he could ask for help; they were all suspects. He could go back and ask Armstrong, but he knew the sheriff would plead his manpower shortage again. Maybe he should try to find Elise's fiancé. No, from the look on her face last night, that subject was off-limits between them. Besides, Alex had no idea how to find the man, even if he was staying nearby.

Alex would just have to hurry through his list of errands and get back to Hatteras West. When it came right down to it, he didn't trust anybody else to make sure Elise remained safe.

The rain had tapered off to a fine mist by the time Alex drove the three miles to the hospital, but the overhead clouds were still filled with dark, ominous shades of black. It looked like they were in for one whale of a storm.

Alex pulled into the hospital parking lot and hurried inside. The hallway leading to the Intensive Care Unit was crawling with kids and adults. Alex overheard someone mumbling about a drive-by shooting, and realized that the victims must have been brought in sometime last night. He looked around, but didn't see Sergeant Hicking anywhere. It was just as well; Alex was in no mood to talk to the SBI agent. He tried looking into the IC unit for Emma, but the curtains had all been fully drawn.

An older nurse stood guard at the desk, and Alex approached her through the crowd of people. "Excuse me, I'd like to check on the status of one of your patients. Her name is Emma Sturbridge."

The nurse looked at him silently, then down at a list posted at the desk. "There's no Sturbridge here."

A trickle of dread danced down Alex's spine. "What exactly does that mean?"

The nurse, having gone back to her paperwork, said, "She's not here. I can say it slower for you if you'd like me to."

"She didn't die, did she?"

Alex couldn't bear the thought of another guest dying.

From behind him, Alex heard someone calling his name. It was Theresa DeAngelis, the nurse he'd talked to the day before. She said, "It looks like your friend is going to be just fine. I called the inn and spoke with a young woman there. She assured me she'd pass the massage along to you."

"Where's Emma now?"

"She woke up a few hours ago complaining of a headache and being hungry. Her doctor decided she was well enough to move to a semiprivate room. It looks like there's a good chance she's going to recover completely."

Alex thanked her for the good news, then hurried off toward the front desk. Emma Sturbridge was awake! He hadn't expected such great news today, and suddenly he'd gotten two positive pieces of information: Emma's improvement coupled with Junior's release. Now if he could just figure out who killed Reg Wellington, maybe he would complete the run. Alex believed that Sam Finster's killer was the same man who'd cut Reg down, but if he started digging into reasons the real estate man might have been murdered he'd be busy until well into the next decade just interviewing the suspects.

After tracking down Emma's room number from the front desk, Alex knocked gently on the door and heard a muffled voice inviting him in.

Emma Sturbridge was sitting up in her bed, looking better than Alex had even hoped. Only one slim tube disappeared into her arm, and her face had that same ruddy complexion Alex had seen the day he'd met her.

Looking farther into the room, Alex saw that Emma was not alone. Mor Pendleton was standing by the corner window. He was watching Alex, but then looked quickly away.

Alex said to him, "I'm surprised to find you here. Have you retired from Mor or Les's?"

Mor shrugged and frowned at his feet. "Well, I felt kind of responsible for Emma, since I was the one who brought her in. I've been checking on her quite a bit, just to make sure she was going to be okay."

Emma smiled. "And now I have two men visiting, with me still in my pajamas." Her grin took on mighty proportions. "I should get pushed off a rock more often."

Alex walked to the bed. "You *were* pushed then? Did you happen to see who did it?"

Emma looked perplexed. "No, and that's the funny part. The whole incident is still fuzzy in my mind."

Alex looked over at Mor as she said it. It seemed to him that the man had more than a casual interest in the matter.

She added, "It's odd though, there is one thing I remember, but it's almost too silly to mention."

Alex pressed her, leaning over the bed. "Whatever it was, you can tell me. It could be a clue as to who might have pushed you."

Emma smiled slightly. "Okay, I'll tell you if you promise not to laugh. I could swear it felt like a tree branch was nudging me over the rock."

Alex said, "A tree? You mean like a branch caught by the wind or something?" There were no trees around Bear Rocks. In fact, one interpretation of the name was that the original designation had been Bare Rocks until someone had started seeing bears in the granite formations.

Emma said, "Wipe that expression off your face, Alex, I know there aren't any trees up there. But that image is stuck in my mind. A tree branch pushed me. Now imagine that."

Mor coughed gently and walked to the other side of

Emma's bed. "I've got to be going, but I'll try to make it back sometime this evening."

Emma turned on her brightest smile for the fix-it man. "I'll be counting the minutes."

After Mor left, Emma said, "Now that fellow is a man I could wrap my arms around. Seems to be interested in me, if I read these visits correctly. The nurse in Intensive Care said he had to be thrown out last night, he was hovering around the station so much!"

That was news to Alex. Mor hadn't seemed all that interested in Emma when Alex had talked to him before. Alex wondered if Mor could have been the one to push her off that rock. It would explain him finding her so fast, and also the fact that he was hovering so close to her hospital bed. If she did happen to remember that Mor had been the one who'd pushed her, he could finish the job he'd started earlier. For that matter, he could have stabbed Reg, too. While Alex hadn't seen him at the inn earlier, Mor could have parked in the woods and walked up one of the trails that covered the property. Finster wouldn't have been any harder for the powerful man to kill. The "why" of it just didn't make any sense.

Alex looked up from his thoughts to see Emma staring intently at him. "You've got something on that mind of yours. Anything you want to talk about?"

Alex didn't know how to address that particular question. If he was right about Mor, he could warn Emma. But if he wasn't, it would make him look like a fool.

Instead of a direct reply, Alex asked, "Is there a buzzer around here in case you need a nurse?"

Emma pointed to a button pinned to her sheet. "Here on the bed. Why do you ask?"

"How fast do they come when you push it?"

Emma looked perplexed by the sudden shift in questioning, but she explained, "I've only pressed it once, but the nurse was here in a few seconds. She said it was because I was so close to the station desk. Now what is this about, Alex?"

"I don't mean to alarm you, but whoever pushed you off that rock might come back to finish the job. If they do, I want help close by."

Emma laughed. "Who in the world would want me that badly? I can't imagine why someone would want to kill me. My ex-husband, perhaps, but he doesn't know I'm here. It all sounds so silly."

"You're in here, aren't you?"

His words had a sobering effect on her. "I can't hide forever, Alex. If it's my time, I'm ready to go."

Great. He'd managed to put out the sun in her eyes all by himself. "Just be careful, okay?"

She added with a subdued smile, "Don't worry so much about me, Alex. If I do go, I plan to take an honor guard with me. Tell you what I will do, though. Whenever someone comes into the room, no matter who it is, I'll keep my finger on the buzzer. Does that satisfy you?"

Alex patted her hand gently. "I wouldn't want anything to happen to you. Watch yourself."

"I promise. Now why don't you let me get some rest? I'm suddenly quite tired."

From the strain on her face, Alex could see that the words were true. After he left, he found a bench in the corridor outside Emma's room and sat down, debating on what to do next. It hadn't been the brightest thing in the world to do, giving a sick woman more things to worry about. He should have called Armstrong instead and persuaded him to put a deputy on the hospital room door. But he already knew what the sheriff's reaction would be, and he didn't particularly want to hear the man's reasons. Besides, the sheriff had apparently given up on doing any work on the case until the full SBI team got to Elkton Falls. If anybody was going to untangle this mess before then, it would have to be up to Alex. He only hoped he could figure it out while there was still time.

What did Reg's death, Emma's fall, the fire and Finster's stabbing all have in common? Taken as separate incidents, they could have a thousand different meanings. But that kind of criminal activity around Hatteras West in such a short period of time couldn't be coincidence. There had to be one thread that tied those people and events together, but Alex couldn't figure out what it could be.

18

Alex's grumbling stomach reminded him that he'd missed lunch. Before he could take care of his hunger, he found a pay telephone and called the inn.

Elise answered on the second ring. Hearing her say, "Hatteras West" brought a smile to his face.

Alex said, "I wanted to let you know that I just saw Emma Sturbridge. She's awake and doing fine."

"Oh, Alex, that's wonderful news. Did she say who pushed her?"

"She said it felt like a tree limb gave her a shove."

"But there's no trees out there on the rocks. Unless . . ."

"Unless what? Do you have *any* idea what she was talking about?"

Elise paused, then said, "No, it just doesn't make sense." Elise lowered her voice and added, "I'll see you later, Alex. Dame Matthews is heading this way, and from the scowl on her face, it's not to compliment us on our fine service."

"Good luck. I'll see you later."

Sally Anne was behind the counter at Buck's, wearing a frown instead of her usual smile.

It was just a little after two, so the regular lunch crowd had thinned to a few stragglers. Still, Sally Anne lowered her voice to a whisper when she spoke to Alex. "Have you heard the news?"

Alex found himself whispering, too. "What news?"

Sally Anne's eyes grew large. "They found that awful man Finster dead in his Cherokee."

Alex lifted his voice slightly before Sally Anne shushed him back into a whisper. "It's all around town. The sheriff came by the inn last night and told me. They found him in an orchard near the inn."

Sally Anne's face was white. "Alex, I think Daddy might have done it."

Alex rocked back on his heels. "Why in the world would you say that?"

"He came in late last night acting like something was really bothering him. When I asked him about it, Dad told me not to worry my pretty little head. I *am* worried, though."

Alex thought for a moment. "How could he have known what was going on with Sam Finster? You didn't tell him, did you?"

Sally Anne's lower lip quivered. "No, but when I pressed him last night, he said I wouldn't have to worry about that goon coming after me anymore, so somebody must have said something to him."

My God, it was possible. Everyone in town knew

how Buck felt about his little girl, even if she was twenty years old.

Then Alex let his fertile imagination rest a moment and thought about it as objectively as he could. "Wait a minute, let's think this through. If Finster had been found beaten to death, I might believe your theory, but do you honestly think your father is the type of guy who would stab a grown man in the back of the neck with an ice pick?"

Sally Anne's face regained some of its color. "Alex, you're right. Daddy would never do something like that." Sally Anne added, "I can't tell you how much better I feel now. I'd like to buy you lunch. Is that okay with you?"

"Sounds great. You know what I like."

Sally Anne gave him her brightest smile. "Thanks again, Alex. I could barely get to sleep last night, wondering if Daddy was going to prison."

Alex walked over to a corner booth away from the traffic flow. In such a small town, it was hard to find any place where he could go to be alone, but the booth offered his best chance.

The club sandwich was excellent, but Alex's thoughts were not good for his appetite. His chain of reasoning kept leading him back to Finster. If Alex could find out from Nadine, the realtor's secretary, who the prospective buyer was, then the pieces might all fit together. Deep in his gut, Alex believed that Hatteras West itself held the key to all his questions.

After thanking Sally Anne for the meal, he decided it was time to visit Finster's office. He only hoped that Nadine had come in to work today to accept condolences for her late boss.

As he started to open the realty office door it was suddenly jerked out of his grasp by someone trying to exit. Alex was stunned to see that it was Joel Grandy.

"Mr. Grandy? What are you doing here?"

The older man looked the slightest bit guilty. "Wanted to offer my condolences."

"I wasn't even aware that you knew Finster."

Grandy stared at Alex for a few moments, then swept through the door without answering.

Nadine was behind her desk, blotting a tissue to her eyes. Now somewhere in her early sixties, Nadine Crowley had been Alex's fifth-grade teacher, and in his mind she hadn't changed a bit. She'd taken an early retirement to be with her husband, but during her retirement party at the school Thad had dropped dead with a massive coronary. When Nadine had tried to get reinstated, the school board apologized but said the papers had already been processed and a new teacher had been hired to take her place. To keep from going crazy, she'd gone back to work. The only job in town that had been open was a secretarial position for Sam Finster. It had taken Alex years to stop referring to her as Mrs. Crowley and start calling her Nadine, as she had so often insisted.

"Nadine, that man who was just here. Mind telling me what he wanted?"

Nadine's voice still had the sharp edge she'd used to such good effect in the classroom. "Now what type of greeting is that, young man?"

Alex stiffened his spine. "I'm sorry, Ma'am, but we've been having a little trouble out at Hatteras West. I think he might be involved."

Nadine Crowley swabbed the tissue at her eyes again

before answering. Alex broke in, "Excuse me for saying so, but surely you couldn't have been that fond of Finster."

She frowned slightly, then added a smile of apology. "You know better than to speak ill of the dead, Alex. But confidentially, I'm not all that sorry to see him go."

"Then why the tears?"

"Young man, feel blessed that you haven't been afflicted with allergies. My eyes have been like this for two weeks. I just can't stand all of the allergens in the air."

That explained the grieving secretary.

"Now, would you mind telling me what Joel Grandy was doing here?"

Nadine said primly, "Not that it's any business of yours, but the fellow appears to be sweet on me. He keeps telling me I'm a dead ringer for his dearly departed spouse. I'll tell you, it's not the kind of compliment a girl dreams of getting, but then again, it's better on average than what I've been managing lately."

Of all the people in the world Alex could trust, Nadine Crowley had to be at the top of his list. Her integrity was known throughout seven counties.

Alex pushed a little more. "So he wasn't checking on any real estate deals?"

Nadine laughed. "Why heavens no. I happened to be eating lunch at Buck's on his first day in town. He spotted me and offered to treat me to a meal. I thought he was cute, so I let him. Joel Grandy's been over here like a love-sick puppy ever since."

Alex thought that might explain why Grandy had made the offer on Hatteras West. It could have been just his effort to stay close to Nadine. "Would you mind telling me something else?"

Nadine's eyes lit up. "Anything."

"Someone's been trying to buy the inn for some time now, but Finster refused to tell me who the buyer was. I'd really like to know."

Nadine Crowley raised her index finger and waved it in front of Alex's face. "I'm not at all certain I have any right to tell you."

"Who's going to know? The name might be important in helping me find out who killed my guest and burned down part of my place."

"I was so sorry to hear about that, Alex." She shuffled a few papers on her desk, then said, "I suppose it doesn't matter now, but I still want you to swear you won't tell anyone I told you."

Alex nodded solemnly. "I promise."

Nadine went to the file cabinet and started searching through the files. After a few minutes, she looked at Alex and said, "I don't understand this. The file's missing."

"Are you sure? Maybe it's somewhere else. Misfiled, maybe?"

Nadine said, "Come now, Alex, I don't misplace or misfile anything. Let me look on his desk."

She came back a full minute later. "It's not there, either. He must have had it with him last night."

So the murderer had taken the evidence after killing Finster. "And you don't have any idea who was after Hatteras West?"

"If I knew, dear boy, I'd tell you. But Sam Finster played things close to the vest. He never even mentioned that someone was making an offer for your inn, though I'd heard plenty of rumors around town about it."

Alex left, knowing he had just run into another dead end.

Walking from Finster's office to the truck, Alex decided to detour one block and see if Mor Pendleton was in. He had a few questions for the man. The last person in the world Alex wanted to suspect was Mor, but too many things had been going on lately for him not to be aware of his friend's ties to recent events.

Mor wasn't in the shop, but Les was. Alex found him sitting at his workbench with his feet propped up. Seven years earlier, Les Williamson had been forced to retire at the age of sixty-five from his regular job as a maintenance man. It had galled Les that he'd been too old to work anywhere but in a business of his own. Taking the largest chunk of his retirement money, he opened the shop just hoping to keep busy until he died. No one had been more surprised than Les that so many of the townsfolk had personal possessions they would rather fix than throw away. Business had been so good that Les had hired Mor, and as the two men grew closer, they'd become partners in the operation.

The older man was reading the latest issue of *Soldiers of the World*, one of his numerous magazine subscriptions. Les had more magazines coming into the shop than the library and the newsstand put together, and he could often be found fighting to catch up with his issues in his free time.

"Is Mor around?"

Les looked up, the strong shop light glaring off his bald head. "Eh? Oh, hello, Alex. No, he's over at the hospital with that Sturbridge woman. I'm telling you, it's getting to be a regular thing, him being gone. It's tough running this place all by myself."

Alex gestured to the magazine and laughed. "I can see you're swamped."

"Just taking a break, boy. Man, some of the things people are fool enough to buy."

"What do you mean?"

Les beckoned him closer, laying the magazine down on the cleared workbench.

"Like this stuff here. This whole page is full of gimmick merchandise. Lethal weapons that look like everyday things. Here's a ring that dispenses poison, and look at this . . ."

The rest of Les's words were lost on Alex. At the bottom of the page was an item for sale that he had seen all too recently. Suddenly, the mystery of the murders at Hatteras West became clear: not the motives, but definitely who was behind the reign of terror.

Alex mumbled his apologies to Les as he tore out of the store. With a deep, sinking feeling in his heart, Alex hoped he could get back to Hatteras West before the killer had a chance to strike again.

19

The drive back to the inn was maddeningly slow for Alex. A pickup truck in front of him loaded with bales of fresh hay drove ten miles under the speed limit, hogging just enough of the road so that Alex couldn't pass him. Alex's thoughts weren't for his own safety; all he could think about was how foolish he'd been to leave Elise at the inn alone. Cursing himself as a fool, Alex fought to keep his driving under control. Running off the road and wrecking wouldn't do Elise the slightest bit of good.

Finally, after a trip that seemed to take hours instead of minutes, he made it back to the inn.

Everything looked calm on the grounds of Hatteras West, though the rain clouds still threatened to break loose at any moment.

After a harried search of the inn, Alex couldn't find a single soul there. Could the killer be at Bear Rocks, or maybe on one of the trails? Was Elise in danger even as he searched for her? If Elise had gone with him into town, she wouldn't be in jeopardy now.

He dialed the sheriff's phone number with a shaking hand, but Armstrong's line was busy, and Alex couldn't spare even a few more seconds in his search for Elise.

Alex ran down the porch stairs and hurried toward the trail to Bear Rocks. As he did, he glanced up at the top observation platform of the lighthouse.

A quiver of fear ran down his spine. There, in the fading light of dusk, he could see two people facing each other in what looked like a heated confrontation on the narrow top balcony. From the dim outlines, Alex figured one of the two figures as the killer. The other looked like Elise. Alex only prayed he wouldn't be too late.

It felt like each of the two hundred sixty eight steps tried to impede his progress as he ran to the summit of the lighthouse. By the time Alex had raced up to the watch room just below the observation deck, his heart felt as if it was going to explode in his chest. Taking only a moment to rest against the smooth plastered wall, Alex approached the smaller set of steps that led to the upper balcony of the lighthouse and listened carefully. From where he stood, he could hear the murderer ranting at Elise.

Fighting to calm his shaking nerves, Alex crept up the ladder carefully, hoping to remain unseen. A sense of relief flooded through him as he realized the murderer was facing toward the mountains! It left Elise in a vulnerable position with her back toward the scanty iron railing that circled the very top of the tower, but it was the chance Alex needed.

The killer was prodding her closer to the edge of the railing with something that looked like a short steel spear. In the distance a bolt of lightning flashed, illuminating the sky with its forked prongs.

Elise must have seen his movements in the flash of lightning as he climbed up the last step. Before he could warn her, Elise's face registered his presence. Alex wasn't the only one to spot her startled expression in the next lightning flash.

The murderer spun around toward him.

"So you finally figured it out."

Alex joined them on the upper platform, keeping a safe distance.

He said, "You were clever, but some of the events around here finally became clear. Why did you kill Reg, Mrs. Matthews?"

The old woman spat out a curse. "The old fool had been watching me from this damn tower every day on my explorations. I knew he was going to steal my claim, so I had to get rid of him. It was ridiculously easy to kill him; he was a weak old man."

Elise spoke over the growing force of the wind. Her voice was calmer than Alex expected. "What claim? I still don't know what you're talking about. I don't even know why you want to kill me."

Barb Matthews turned back to Elise, and for a split second Alex considered jumping her and wrestling the deadly shaft out of her hands. But he hesitated a moment too long before acting, and the old woman pressed the blade closer to Elise's chest. It was an exact duplicate of the stiletto-bladed cane Alex had just seen in Les's catalogue.

Barb Matthews snapped, "I'm warning you, Alex, if you try anything, she's going to die."

He backed up a few steps.

"That's better," she said. "Do you want to tell her what's going on, or shall I?"

Alex said, "I can give it a try; I've figured most of it out. Somehow you have the impression there's a deposit of precious stones around here. You must have heard about my great-grandfather."

The Matthews woman snorted. "I heard about him all right. Those original jewels were found right here on this property, weren't they?"

Alex looked at the woman in shock. "Are you insane? Why would I sit on a fortune in gems and not do anything about it? It just doesn't make any sense."

A look of doubt crossed Barb Matthews's face, then dissipated as quickly as it had come. "Okay, you didn't know the truth yourself. But there are precious stones here. I have proof!" She reached into her pocket with one hand and pulled out a handful of small green stones. "I found these emerald chips during my first visit here. They're genuine, I had them tested. And where there are chips, there are whole gems nearby!"

Alex said, "You found these on the property! They were salted."

A burst of cold fury escaped the older woman's lips. "What are you talking about?"

"My father thought a few gem-finds on our land would increase the tourist trade. When Mom found out about what he'd done, she hit the roof. So Dad backed down and retrieved all the stones he could remember planting in the landscape. Evidently he missed quite a few."

Barb Matthews hissed, "That's impossible. You're lying."

Elise said, "It's true. Alex told me about it a couple of days ago."

In a fit of rage, the slight older woman lunged at Elise with the palm of her free hand and shoved her over the rail! As she fell, Alex prayed she would stay close to the tower instead of cartwheeling over, since the lower balcony extended out farther than the upper one. He heard a ringing thud as Elise made contact with the platform below. It was still a ten-foot fall, and Alex knew it was enough to seriously hurt her if she hit at the wrong angle, but at least she had a fighting chance.

In desperation, Alex dove for Barb Matthews. He was too far away, and she managed to keep her hold on the blade. Alex saw the sharp point gleaming in another flash of lightning as she raised the weapon toward his chest. The wind assaulted him with growing fury, but Alex was so focused on the blade that was poised to skewer him, that he barely registered the wind's presence.

He yelled, "What are you going to do, kill everyone who suspects you?"

Barb Matthews seemed to think about that very thing for a moment. "There's still a way out for me. Even if you're telling the truth and this property is as worthless as you think it is, I won't have to go to jail. No one would believe that a little old woman like me would be capable of murder, and with you gone, there won't be anyone left who suspects me."

Alex said, "Why did you drag Elise into this? It doesn't make any sense."

"I lured your maid up here because I was sure she'd found my emeralds. You know I told you people not to clean my room, but she did it anyway. I convinced her you were up here waiting for her. You should have seen the little fool rush up to be with you. It was pathetic."

Alex felt sick about having been used as bait. "You'll never get away with this."

Barb Matthews laughed. "I've already got my story ready. Two secret lovers in a double suicide leap off the lighthouse tower. The press will eat it up." She shook her head in disgust. "I should have killed you first. I know your brother would have sold me the property the second after he inherited it from you. That fact is obvious enough by the way your father's estate was settled." She frowned, then added, "That would have to be better than working through that idiot Finster."

Alex said, "Killing Finster with your cane was what gave you away. I figured you were trying to cover up your trail. And you burned down the main keeper's quarters to force me into selling, didn't you? I started wondering why someone would want to buy a less valuable piece of property, but you never were interested in the buildings, just the ground they stood on."

"When you wouldn't give in, I decided to take matters into my own hands and speed things along. You're not as bright as I gave you credit for."

Alex had to stall until he could come up with a way to disarm her. "You thought Reg was spying on you, but how about Emma Sturbridge? Why did you push her off Bear Rocks?"

Barb Matthews spoke to Alex as if he were a child.

"I didn't want anyone to link her death with the others. I still don't know how she survived the fall. In hindsight, I should have stabbed her, too. It's much more efficient."

Alex persisted. "That still doesn't explain why you wanted her dead."

"The fool woman was going to jump my claim. Where do you think I found my emeralds?"

Alex groaned. "Somewhere near Bear Rocks. It's all starting to make sense."

She smiled wickedly. "So you've finally got it." With that, she thrust her blade toward Alex's chest, trying to pin him to the lighthouse itself.

At that precise moment, the Fresnel lens jumped into life above them, spearing Barb Matthews with its powerful beam. Alex lunged for the arm that brandished the deadly cane, but she jerked back instead of driving the blade home. His grab for her missed, as Barb Matthews went over the railing and dropped into the howling darkness. Several seconds later, he heard a muffled cry as her body hit the ground two hundred feet below.

Alex rushed down the narrow stairs and found Elise leaning weakly against the switch that supplied power to the lens. It was a good thing Alex had explained to her how the light operated; there was no doubt in his mind she had kept him from joining Reg in his lighthouse death.

Alex wrapped her in his arms, hugging her with all his might. "Thank God you're all right. Elise, you saved my life."

Elise's voice was muffled. "Take it easy, Alex, I'm pretty sure I broke a rib or two from that fall. We saved each other. If you hadn't come along when you did, she would have either forced me over the edge or stabbed me with that cane. Oh, Alex."

Elise started sobbing into his shoulder. Alex held her as delicately as he could, stroking her hair with his hand.

Softly, he said, "Will you be all right up here by yourself for a few minutes? I want to call an ambulance."

Elise's voice was shaky as she answered. "I can walk down the stairs if I lean on you. I don't think I can handle being alone up here."

Alex wasn't in any mood to argue. They made it down the steps, though slowly. As the two of them stumbled back to the inn, they walked past the crumpled body of Barb Matthews.

She didn't look like a killer.

When he thought about how close she'd come to killing both of them, Alex shivered.

For once, he didn't mind hearing the sirens of the ambulance and the police cruiser as they raced toward Hatteras West.

20

Two weeks later, Alex, Elise, Mor and Emma were at the lake, enjoying a picnic near the placid waters. Alex had built a fire near the edge of the shore; the fresh pops and crackles of wood burning accented shimmering reflections of the flames on the water.

Alex broke the silence. "It's hard to believe you're out of the hospital already, Emma."

Emma Sturbridge sat against a tree watching the fire and the water. A discreet bandage on the back of her head offered the only sign of her recent brush with death, though the doctors had told her to take things easy for a while.

Emma laughed. "It'll take more than that she-devil to keep me down. You two did me a real favor getting rid of her, though. I'm already sleeping better at night. The nightmares are just about gone."

Mor grinned at her. "From the look of things, you'll be chasing the boys again in no time."

Emma's smile was steady as she replied, "In that case, you'd better get your track shoes out, Mordecai."

Alex laughed when he saw his old friend's smile vanish. Mor abruptly changed the subject. "Anybody else ready to head up to the inn? I'd like a drink before I go home. It's getting kind of cool out here."

Emma said, "I *would* like to get back to that sofa. Do you two mind?"

Elise stood up. "I'm ready, too. Are you coming, Alex?"

"Let me douse this first." He threw a bucket of lake water onto the flames and was rewarded with a billowing cloud of smoke and the loud hiss of the dying fire.

Soon they were back at the inn, settled comfortably in the lobby. Alex couldn't sit still. After lighting the stacked wood in the fireplace, he stood at the mantle and watched the fire take hold.

Elise applauded the flames. "Two fires in one night. I love it."

Alex said, "I'd like to say it's just to take the chill off, but I've got to admit, it's nice having a fire in the autumn." The inn was closed for lack of guests. Barb Matthews was dead, Junior was in town working on the sheriff's campaign and Joel Grandy had persuaded Nadine to go on a trip with him to the Florida Keys. Alex had canceled the few upcoming reservations he'd had in order to figure out what he was going to do next.

As he stared at the fire, Alex retrieved a brandy snifter full of unpolished stones that sat on the mantle. Shifting the glass in his hand, he swirled the rough rocks around gently, as if they were fine cognac. The SBI had recovered the stones from Barb Matthews's pockets after she'd fallen. Since their intrinsic value appeared to be rather small and the woman had no known living relatives, Sheriff Armstrong had decided that the gems should stay at the lighthouse as a testament to the week's events, and Hicking had agreed.

Alex said, "To think this entire mess started because of a prank my dad pulled twenty years ago."

He lightly fingered a few of the stones in the snifter and then returned the glass to the mantle.

Emma stretched out her hands for the glass. "Those are the stones they recovered off that awful woman's body? Let me see them a minute, Alex." She studied the rocks carefully in the flickering light of the fireplace, then asked excitedly for the house lights to be turned on. Alex complied, wondering if his new friend had completely recovered from her head injury.

Emma snapped, "Mor, go get that magnifying glass for me, would you? It's over on the counter." He obeyed without a word, and Alex realized Mor was a little intimidated by the vibrant woman.

When Emma spoke again, there was a hint of wonder in her voice. "Alex, you said your dad salted the area with emerald chips."

"That's right. It's in Mom's diary. I looked the entry up after Elise and I talked about it. Thank God it was in the attic over here and not in the main keeper's quarters. At least I didn't lose everything."

Emma pushed on. "No other stones? Just emeralds?"

"As far as I know, that's it. It's turned into some kind of family legend. What's on your mind, Emma?"

There was a huge smile on Emma's face. "I'll be. I was right after all. This area is another vein location for some pretty nice stones."

She held a pretty rock up to the light. "Do you see

this? It's tourmaline. And this one is garnet. Hey, here's a pretty nice sapphire." She held a green stone to the light. "Your father never salted this emerald, it's worth a fortune! Alex, unless I've missed my guess completely, Barb Matthews could have been right after all. This property was the only place she looked for stones, wasn't it?"

"She never left the grounds. You really think there are precious stones on my land?"

Emma's smile was genuine. "I would have to believe that your inn is saved. It looks like your great-grandfather had a real knack for choosing his land."

"Well I'll be." Alex laughed heartily. "Dad would have loved it. He salted an area that already had precious stones on it!"

"That's what it looks like. Now all you've got to do is find the veins and start digging."

Alex shook his head. "That can wait until you're better. You can have the job if you want it, on one condition. I want you to recover what you can as discreetly as possible. After all, I don't want to open up a mine. I *like* running an inn."

"That sounds like a fine offer. I accept," she said as she looked steadily at Mor.

Alex motioned gently to Elise, and they walked out together onto the porch. They had an excellent view of the lighthouse from where they stood.

Alex said heavily, "I guess you'll be leaving us now."

"Why do you say that?"

He stammered, "I just assumed, you know, with Peter coming here and all . . ."

Elise said softly, "I'm staying, Alex."

"What about Peter?"

"What about him?" Elise asked pointedly. "I've decided to stay, unless you don't want me here."

"No, that's not it at all. You can work at Hatteras West as long as you want."

He couldn't believe it!

Was there a chance Elise was staying at Hatteras West to be close to him? He fought the urge to tell her he'd broken up with Sandra. On the heels of her decision to stay, it might look as if he was pressing her.

No, Alex would bide his time and wait for the right moment to come along.

Though its beacon was dark, the light of a full moon gave the lighthouse lens a soft, gentle glow above them. As a fleeting cloud passed over the moon, the lighthouse seemed to wink at him, offering its approval.